# The Lustful Turk

By Anonimasu Tokumeikibou    Illustrated By Shin Reiki

Western
Ranobe
Dark

# Western Ranobe
## DARK

# Victorian
# Taboo

9 781939 977977

Or Scenes in the Harem of an Eastern Potentate faithfully and vividly depicting in a series of letters from a young and beautiful English lady to her friend in England the full particulars of her ravishment and of her complete abandonment to all the salacious tastes of the Turks, the whole being described with that zest and simplicity which always gives guarantee of authenticity.

Letter 1

Emily Barlow to Sylvia Carey

Portsmouth, Crown Hotel

18 June 1814

Dearest Sylvia,

We arrived here early this morning after a most melancholy journey. Time alone can remove the painful impressions which the appearance of poor Henry created as we parted. Never shall I forget the picture of despair he exhibited. Do all you can to comfort him, tell him although I obey my mother's and my uncle's wishes, still my heart in every clime will be true to him. Poor Eliza did everything in her power on the road to this place to amuse my wounded feelings, but it was beyond the extent of her artless sophistry to remove the weight that pressed upon my heart. Oh, Sylvia! How cruel is the sacrifice exacted in our obedience to our parents; how happy had I been if this uncle of mine had never existed! My mother, my friend, my lover— all, all I hold dear—sacrificed to the prospect of possessing this uncle's wealth. Heaven knows how fondly I dwelt upon the hopes of shortly becoming the happy wife of your brother, you may guess (but I pray that you may never feel) the anguish caused by such a separation. But it is decided. I can now only supplicate heaven for a speedy return. On our arrival we found the captain of the Indiaman anxiously expecting us. The wind having been fair for some hours, if we had not appeared as we did, he would have sailed without us; truly happy should I have been if he had; and if I had known that a trifling delay on the road would have prevented our departure, I most certainly would have created it.

Adieu, my dear Sylvia, a long adieu. The boat waits to convey us on board at the Momerbank, as the captain calls it Farewell, Sylvia, comfort poor Henry, when I think of him I feel what it is impossible to describe.

Your unhappy friend,

EMILY BARLOW

Letter 2

Ali, Dey of Algiers, to Muzra, Dey of Tunis

20 September 1814.

Muzra, thy friend greets thee, with thanks for thy late present. I allude to the Grecian maid (for so she was) you sent me with the treasure. The bearer of this dispatch has the care of a pair of beautiful stallions which I lately captured from a tribe of Askulites; they made an inroad into a part of my territories from the desert, but I came upon them by surprise, and properly chastised their presumption: not more than a hundred escaped out of two thousand; indeed I was in no humour to spare them, they having disturbed me in a scene of pleasure, for which mere could be no pardon, but more of this hereafter. The Grecian slave, I rejoice to say again, I found a pure maid; her virginity I sacrificed on the Beiram feast of our Holy Prophet. To cull her sweet flower, I was obliged to infuse an opiate in her coffee. Again, and again, I thank you for the present—her beauties are indeed luxurious; in her soft embraces I find a sure solace from my anxieties of state, but how strange it is, Muzra, that these slaves, whose destinies depend on our will, rarely give that fervent return to our pleasure so absolutely necessary to the full voluptuous energy of enjoyment. It is true nature will always exert its power over the softer sex, and they frequently give way to its excitement, but the pleasure they experience is merely animal. Thus it is with Zena (so I have named your present): even in the height of our ecstasies, a cloud seems to hang on her beauteous countenance, clearly indicating that it is nature, not love, that creates her transport. This knowledge considerably diminishes the enjoyment her beauties afford me, yet still she has become extremely necessary to my pleasures. Although the novelty of her charms has gone by, the certainty of having cropped her virgin rose has created a lasting interest in my bosom, which the dissolving luster and modest, bashful expression of her eyes daily increases—indeed her charms frequently entice me from the arms of another beauty, whom I may say for these last two months I have continually enjoyed without me least abatement of my ardour—on the contrary, my appetite seems to increase by what I feed on. It is true when I think of the pensive charms of Zena I devote a few hours to her arms, but she only acts like the whetstone to the knife, and sends me back to the embraces of my English slave with re-doubled vigour and zest. In my next dispatch I will give you an account of my becoming possessed of this girl, who has so enchanted thy friend's desires. May our Prophet have thee in his holy keeping.

ALI

Letter 3

Sylvia Carey to Emily Barlow

London, 19 June

Fare thee well, dear Emily, and a safe voyage is the nightly prayer of your now lonely friend. I received your letter of yesterday, and hope you will receive this before you sail. Poor Henry has only been once out of his room since your departure. I will not shock you with an account of his wretchedness, but be assured nothing will be left undone to relieve his sufferings, though I tremble for the result; your mother saw him today, she was much shocked at his dejection; but I trust time will do much, and that you may yet be happy in the possession of each other. The providence that separates may again join. It is useless to despond. Take every opportunity of writing to us, by every ship you meet on your passage! God bless you.

SYLVIA CAREY

(This letter Emily never received, the ship having sailed before it arrived at Portsmouth.)

# Letter 4

Emily Barlow to Sylvia Carey

Algiers, 24 July 1814


Dearest Sylvia—

I think I see the expression of surprise you experience on perceiving my letter dated from this place. Oh, God, Sylvia, to what a wretched fate has the intended kindness of my uncle devoted your miserable unfortunate friend. Pity me, Sylvia; pity my wretchedness. You have no doubt heard of the cruel treatment experienced by females who are unfortunate enough to fall into the power of these barbarous Turks, particularly those who have any pretensions to beauty; but it is utterly impossible for you, Sylvia, to conjecture anything like my sufferings since we parted. I shudder with agony when I look back to what I have been forced to undergo. Pity me, my dear friend. My tears blot out the words nearly as quick as I write them. Oh God, Sylvia, I have no longer any claim to chastity. Surely never was poor maid so unfeelingly deprived of her virtue. The very day the accursed pirate brought me to this place did the Dey, with cruel force, in spite of my entreaties, deprive me of my virginity. In vain I resisted with all the strength nature had bestowed on me. It was no use. In vain I made the harem resound with my cries but no help or assistance came to succour your poor friend; at length, wearied out by struggling in defense of my innocence, my strength at last completely failed me, and my powerful ravisher unrelentingly completed my undoing. Oh, Sylvia, your poor friend is now the polluted concubine of this most worthless Turk.

You no doubt are anxious to hear how I came into his power. The story of my ruin is short. The day after I wrote to you from Portsmouth we sailed down the English Channel with most delightful weather, but in losing sight of land I became extremely seasick, so much so that I could not even crawl upon deck. In this state I continued about three weeks. One day I heard a most unusual noise upon deck, and when I sent Eliza to learn the cause of it, a mate told her that the ship was likely to be attacked by Moorish pirates. You may easily guess our terror at this information, which turned out to be all too true, for shortly the discharge of guns with the shouts of the combatants informed us the work of destruction was begun. The firing continued a considerable time without intermission, and when the discharge of our guns was discontinued, the uproar, cries and groans on the deck became too horrid to describe, or to last long. On a sudden everything became quiet, but a rush we heard coming towards the cabin too surely warned us of our approaching captivity. In an instant the door was burst open, and in rushed a crowd of armed Turks covered with blood. Unable longer to sustain the various emotions with which for the last two hours I had been agitated, and still suffering from the remains of my sickness, I fainted in the arms of Eliza. On recovering my senses I found myself in my berth attended by Eliza, from whom I learned we had been captured by an Algerine corsair, who had ordered every attention to be paid me, and she believed the corsair was making for the Straits of Gibraltar.

In short, about a week after passing Gibraltar, the firing of a salute announced we were under the walls of Algiers; during the passage to this place I was not troubled with any visit from the captain, but immediately the vessel was safely anchored, he came to the cabin, and ordered us in good English to get ourselves ready to go ashore in the course of half an hour.

Hearing him speak English so well, I took this opportunity of enquiring what his intentions were respecting us, but was struck speechless by his answering that his intention was to make a present of us to the Dey! He added he thought I was particularly worthy of that honour. So profound was my horror at this information, that I in vain essayed for several minutes to speak, and had I not found relief in a flood of tears, most certainly my emotions would have been fatal to me. The brute of a captain observed my tears and coolly remarked, 'Oh! Oh! Waterworks! Ah! Ah!' he continued, laughing aloud, 'if you should happen to be a maid, the Dey will make you cry in another way I guess.' He then returned to the deck. I have since learned that this barbarian is an English renegade.

Poor Eliza appeared as much overcome as myself, for in point of personal attractions few girls could be more well-endowed. A strong presentiment of my approaching fate had taken forcible possession of my mind. All Eliza could do or say, brought no relief to my apprehensions. The expiration of this time again brought the captain to the cabin, who, covering us with thick veils, conducted us both on deck. In a few minutes we entered the Watergate of the Dey's harem. It was about half-past six o'clock in the evening of the 12th of this month that I entered this palace, so fatal to my modesty. I had scarcely been in it half an hour ere my virtue received so severe an insult that the complete loss of chastity only could exceed what I suffered. In less than five hours the cruel Dey had thoroughly deprived me of every claim to virginity. But you shall know all, just as it happened. Directly we were in the harem we were rather dragged than led into a most sumptuous chamber, at the far end of which sat the Dey, apparently about forty-five years of age, smoking a peculiar kind of pipe. The captain immediately prostrated himself, and spoke to him in the Turkish language, pointing at the same time to me and Eliza. The Dey surveyed us for a few moments without rising. He then said something to the captain, who rose from his prostrate position, took Eliza by the hand, and led her out of the room. I was about to follow, but was ordered by the captain to remain. Trembling with terror I was forced to obey.

No sooner were the captain and Eliza withdrawn than the Dey rose from the couch, walked leisurely towards me, and laid hold of my hand, which trembled in his grasp. After considering a few moments, he chucked me under the chin and said in good English that Mahomet had been kind in blessing him with so fair a slave as myself. I was not much surprised to hear the Dey speak English, the captain having spoken it so well, but the terror his address gave me cannot be described, and indeed good reason I had for my apprehensions. Directly he had spoken, he began leading me towards the couch, but I instantaneously drew back, on which without further ceremony he caught me around the waist and in spite of the resistance I made, forced me to it; then, seating himself, he drew me to him and forced me to seat myself upon his knees. If it had been in my power to resist, the excess of my confusion alone would have prevented my throwing any effectual obstacle in the way of his proceedings. Directly he had got me thus he threw one of his arms round my neck, and drew my lips to his, closing my mouth with his audacious kisses. Whilst his lips were as it were glued to mine, he forced his tongue into my mouth in a manner which created a sensation it is quite impossible to describe. It was the first liberty of the kind I ever sustained.

You may guess the shock it at first gave me, but you will scarcely credit it when I own that my indignation was not of long continuance. Nature, too powerful nature, had become aroused and assisted his lascivious proceedings, conveying his kisses, brutal as they were, to the inmost recesses of my heart On a sudden, new and wild sensations blended with my shame and rage, which exerted themselves but faintly; in fact, Sylvia, in a few short moments his kisses and his tongue threw my senses into a complete tumult and an unknown fire rushed through every part of me, hurried on by a strange pleasure. All my loud cries dwindled into gentle sighs, and in spite of my inward rage and grief, I could not resist; wanting strength for self-defense, I could only bewail my situation. I told you he had me on his knees, with one of his arms round my neck. Finding how little I resisted, and having me thus with our lips closely joined, his other hand he suddenly thrust under my petticoats. Incensed by this vital insult, I strove to break from his arms, but it was of no use. He held me firm, my cries and reproaches he heeded not! If by my struggles I contrived to free my lips, they were quickly regained again; thus with his hand and his lips he kept me in the greatest disorder, whilst in proportion as it increased I felt my fury and strength diminish. At last a dizzy sensation seized on every sense. I felt his hand rapidly divide my thighs, and quickly one of his fingers penetrated that place which, God knows, no male hand had ever before touched. If anything was wanting to complete my confusion, it was the thrilling sensation I felt, caused by the touches of his finger. What a dreadful moment was this for my virtue! With all the highest notions of the charms of that dear innocence which I was doomed to be so soon deprived of, dreading even in my soul's disorder nothing so much as losing it, how strange then it was that pleasure should not be overcome by such fears. Why did they not instantly snatch me from the pleasure? I wished some help would come to save me from the danger, but I no sooner formed the wish than a kiss and his finger created a contrary emotion, and each following kiss grew more and more pleasing, till at last I almost wished nothing might oppose my absolute defeat. In blushing at what I felt, I blush to write, I longed to feel more. Without an idea what that which I panted for could be, I eagerly awaited the instruction, until the impetu-

ous ardour began to be too powerful for the senses.

Finding that I made no attempt to withdraw my lips from his thrilling pressure, his arm which was around my neck he removed to my waist, thus drawing me more strongly to his bosom; his right arm became closely confined between his body and mine, my hand being placed and held firmly between his thighs. Whilst in this position, I felt something beneath his clothes gradually enlarging and moving against my hand; from the length I felt it against my arm, I judged it to be very long and thick also. If I had wished to remove my hand from its position I could not; and so wonderful was the fascination I felt from the mere touch of this unknown object, I think I could not have removed my hand had it been perfectly at liberty. Without knowing what it was, every throb created in me a tremor unac-countable. I little dreamed the dreadful anguish I was doomed to experience by that which my hand was warming and raising to life.

By this time the Dey had satisfied himself of my being a virgin. Sunk though I was in sensual lethargy, I had not been able to silence an unfortunate monitor within my breast who, though hitherto unsuccessful, was yet reproaching me for my weakness. The Dey, fully perceiving the impression he had made, resolved to take immediate advantage of it. But how shall I describe what I still blush to think of, but it must be done. He withdrew his hand from between my thighs, forced me on my back on the couch, and in an instant turned up my clothes above my navel. Thus all my secret charms became exposed to his view. Exhausted as I was and lost in desire, I could make no further resistance. His hands quickly divided my thighs and he got between them. During my struggles my neckerchief had be-come loose and disordered. He now entirely removed it, leaving my neck and breast quite bare.

Although I could scarcely keep my eyes open from the tumult of my senses, still I could not help observing as he was on his knees between my thighs that he was divesting himself of his lower garments. For the first time in my life I caught a view of that terrible instrument, that fatal foe to virginity. With unutterable sensations I felt his naked glowing body join mine, again my lips were glued to his, softening me to ruin with his inflamed suctions. In a delirium little short of pleasure, panting with desire, I waited my coming fate. (I really think if at this moment he had completed my seduction, I should not have regretted my loss of virtue; but no, it was decreed that on being deprived of my innocence I should be entirely free of all those soft desires he had so powerfully excited, and that I should suffer during my defloration every anguish a maid can feel, personal as well as mental. But to my unfortunate tale.) The Dey had properly fixed himself to do that which I ought but certainly at that moment did not dread. No, even as his daring hand fixed the head of his terrible instrument where his lascivious fingers had so potently assisted in reducing me to my then passive state, I own I felt it even with pleasure stiffly distending my until that moment untouched modesty. But on the very instant when I had willingly resigned everything to what I then considered my fixed destiny, his eyes, whose luster and expression I could scarcely sustain of, on a sudden were filled with languor. He seemed as it were abashed, and kissing me with less violence, he grew by degrees even weaker than myself. Suddenly I felt my thighs overflowed by something warm that spurted in torrents from his instrument. At last he sank in my arms in a kind of trance.

The Day's weakness continuing, my confusion began to dissipate so much that by making an effort I found no difficulty in disengaging myself from his arms. I got off the couch. As I grew composed and capable of recollection, the more I became sensible of my shame, together with the dreadful shock my modesty had experienced. A melancholy seized me. I shuddered at what I was likely to encounter judging by what I had already experienced. However, I returned thanks to heaven for my present escape. By this time I had adjusted my dress and the Dey had done the same thing and, coming up to me, he again placed his arm around my waist. Hardly recovered from my first confusion, I trembled for fear the same scene was again commencing, but fortunately I was deceived. He only kissed my cheek in a manner which had nothing displeasing in it, and said, as well as I can recollect, 'Lovely Christian, it is not the pleasure of our Holy prophet that I should at present be indulged in the enjoyment of your beauties, but when I return from a journey I am about to make, I shall no doubt be able to do justice to your charms. Until my return I shall order everything for your pleasure and amusement. But come,' he continued, 'I will conduct you to the apartment I intend you shall occupy.' I now summoned up courage to address him, although I could scarcely look in his face. I told him my exact situation, of my affection for Henry, that no doubt my uncle would pay a very high ransom if I was released without any further attempts against my virtue. This I threw out to tempt his cupidity, supposing, as I always understood the Algerines to be a most rapacious set of men, the hopes of gaining a large sum would induce him to spare me. He listened very patiently to all I advanced. Encouraged by his attention, I proceeded to add entreaties and supplications supported by tears, but on a sudden he drew me to his bosom and kissed away my tears, replying in these decisive words—'It cannot be; it is in vain you plead; your fate is fixed. I would not part with you for all the treasure of the combined world, let alone what one individual could produce. Do not indulge yourself, lovely one, with any vain hopes of ransom, for if the Commander of the Faithful was to order it, I would not part with you. The delicious odour of your virgin flower is reserved for my enjoyment In a few days I shall return, and then, lovely houri, you must resign yourself without reluctance or coyness to my fierce desires, and in return I will teach you such sweet pleasure that you will soon cease to regret having been thrown in my power. How could you for a moment imagine I should be foolish enough to resign beauties such as yours to the arms of a rival, too? To let a favoured Christian pluck your maiden rose. No, sweet virgin, the soft pleasure is surely reserved for me,' and he drew my lips to his; 'it is I that am doomed to cull the flower. To me belongs the delightful task of transforming you into a finished woman, and cropping that delicate treasure, so much sought after, but so seldom found.' My heart entirely failed me at the decided refusal, and he led me trembling to the apartments I was to occupy. They consisted of a suite of three rooms, situated at the end of a long gallery. As we entered he explained to me the use of each room.


The first was the general apartment for eating or receiving company in, the second for dressing, whilst the third and innermost one was the bedroom; this last could be approached only through the other two rooms—at least so it appeared to me. In the bedroom were three large windows. On examination I found them to look out to the sea, which was beating the walls underneath at a great depth. There was no possibility of any approach or escape on that side. Whilst I was gazing at the shipping in the harbour, the Dey seized my hand and gently drew me towards the bed, which was in one of the corners of the room, made of large velvet cushions in the most magnificent style, after the Eastern fashion. The two sides of the wall which formed the angle in which the bed was placed were entirely covered with looking-glass, as was the ceiling above. A sudden trembling seized me on viewing the fatal bed, which the Dey observing, he took me in his arms and kissing me said, 'On my return I shall soon release you from all these tremblings and fear.' He kept his word, but it was much sooner than I expected or than he promised. After he had pointed out all the conveniences of the room, together with their several uses, he gave me a key, informing me it was the key of my sleeping apartment. He then took me in his arms, covering my lips and neck with kisses, and bid me to expect his return in a week, by which time, he said, he had no doubt of my entire submission to his desires. The way these intimations were given was so peculiar and new to me, combining so much of me authority of a master, that it was entirely out of my power to make any reply, and he left me. The first thing I did when he was gone was to inspect my door of the bedroom. To my great joy I found the lock was on the inside and the key being in my possession I felt comparatively safe.

I next examined the room most attentively, and after a strict searching felt convinced there was no other entrance but the door, it being entirely impossible for anyone to approach by the windows. I was much relieved in mind after this inspection.

Just as I had finished my examination, in came four female slaves whom the Dey had appointed to attend me. One of them spoke English. I enquired of her if I could have Eliza, but was informed me Dey considered her too handsome to be an attendant. At present she was considered one of his mistresses, and would remain so if she was found worthy of that honour by being still a maid. This information caused me to sigh for poor Eliza. The slaves now brought all kinds of refreshments, of which I stood much in need.

After dinner I retired to the bedroom, and seated myself on a couch in one of the recesses of the windows; the prospect was beautiful; the sun had just sunk on me western horizon behind the white terraces of the city but still there was sufficient light to discern everything going on in the harbour, and on the mole—indeed the scene was delightful; for a few moments my unfortunate state was forgotten. I was disturbed by the slave who spoke English bringing in a parcel of English books, with a silver bell to ring should I want anything. Whilst she was in the room a discharge of guns took place from the castle and batteries, and she informed me that whenever the Dey left or returned to the city he was always saluted in that way. She further added he was not expected to return for a fortnight. Feeling assured I should not be troubled by the Dey for some time, and finding myself much overcome from what I had undergone, I rang for lights, determined to retire to bed. Directly they understood my intentions, the slaves came round me for the purpose of undressing me, but I commanded them to retire, which they did, after placing everything for my service. I then locked the door, determined on again searching the room; still finding nothing to create any fear, I proceeded to undress myself, but at the very moment I had taken off my chemise, preparatory to putting on night linen, you may guess my terror on hearing a noise by the side of the bed. Ere I could have turned my head I found myself in the arms of the Dey, who was as naked as myself. Oh, God! You cannot imagine my terror and despair at this moment. You see how I was lulled into security that I might become an easy victim. I felt assured the Dey had left Algiers—the firing of the guns, the slave's account, was all trumped up to lull me to my ruin, all invented to throw me off my guard; in short, he allowed me no time for reflection. Defenseless and naked in his arms, I was carried to the bed and thrown down on it. My shrieks must have been heard through the palace but no help was nigh to prevent my ruin. What could a feeble maid like myself effect against so powerful an antagonist? Nothing—for in less time than it takes to write it, he forcibly extended my thighs and placed himself between them. Oh, God! Even now, when it is all over, and recompensed as I have most certainly been for my sufferings, I tremble at the bare recollection of the dreadful anguish I suffered when he reduced my chastity to a bleeding ruin. I soon found it was useless to struggle or resist, I was a mere child in his arms; as to strength, he moved and placed me just as was convenient to his pleasure. I quickly felt his finger again introducing the head of that terrible engine I had before felt, and which now felt like a pillar of ivory entering me.

Directly he had secured its head within me, he withdrew his hand, placed his arm round my neck, and drew my lips to his. At this moment I was nearly insensible to everything he did, so much were my feelings overcome by fear and shame. But I was not doomed to remain long in this state, for I quickly felt him forcing his way into me, with a fury that caused me to scream with anguish. My petitions, supplications and tears were of no use. I was on the altar, and, butcher-like, he was determined to complete the sacrifice; indeed, my cries seemed only to excite him to the finishing of my ruin, and sucking my lips and breasts with fury, he unrelentingly rooted up all obstacles my virginity offered, tearing and cutting me to pieces, until the complete junction of our bodies announced that the whole of his terrible shaft was buried within me. I could bear the dreadful torment no longer: uttering a piercing cry I sank insensible in the arms of my cruel ravisher. How long I continued in this happy state of insensibility, I know not, but I was brought back to life feeling the same thrilling agony which caused my fainting. Still grasped in his arms, I felt him moving up and down upon me with a force and energy that made me feel every motion of the instrument which I was impaled upon like the cutting of a knife. Every thrust he made was followed by some ejaculation, such as, 'Delicious creature, how tight she is! Holy Mahomet, I thank you. Oh! Ah! Who would be without it. There sweet infidel,' as he drove himself up to the hilt in me, with many other words in the Turkish language which I did not understand, until the fury of his thrusts became so cruelly savage that I a second time fainted.

 

Stretched beyond bearing, as I may say I was, by the instrument of my martyrdom before my second fainting, I now in spite of my suffering could not help being considerably surprised at the very great alteration I experienced, although I most sensibly felt it, but still it had lost most of that fierce stiffness with which it first tore me to pieces. Whilst my mind was thus occupied with reflections on this novel change, my astonishment was augmented by feeling it as it were, by degrees, assuming all its former strength and erection within me, while the Dey was amusing himself with sucking my lips, me nipples of my breasts, and arranging my hair over my shoulders and bosom, in various ways to please his fancy, also moving my face into different positions, as he said, to see which way it appeared the most lovely—until the return of the same cruel distention of the parts painfully informed me his instrument had recovered its fierce condition. The Dey now withdrew it all but the head, which he left between the lips of the sheath, which it had so lately formed for itself, and having with his hand satisfied himself as to its strength for performing the third assault, he withdrew his hand and keeping me firmly to his bosom, at one tremendous thrust drove it up into me, distending the tender, wounded and torn parts, until the mutual mixture of our hair stopped his further progress. He now lay for some time quiet in my arms, to all appearance from his various exclamations swimming in a sea of pleasure, sucking my breast and neck, until they became quite sore; all the time I lay gasping and stretched beyond bearing. Soon again I felt me commencement of his dreadful thrusts—at first, to be sure, they were not quite so fierce; but as his feelings were excited by enjoyment, so did the fury of his movements increase. I could not restrain my cries, and just at the moment his lunges were creating an anguish intolerable, a loud knocking at his door caused the Dey to jump from my arms. So dreadful was the anguish from the sudden way in which the cause of my suffering was withdrawn from me, that I again fainted. When I recovered, I found myself tying in the arms of the Dey, who was anxiously watching over me. He then informed me that the disturbance which had forced him so precipitately to leave my embraces was occasioned by one of his eunuchs coming to inform him of a sudden invasion of part of his territories by some Arabs which rendered it necessary he should immediately proceed to join his troops; but he swore by his Prophet severely to chastise them for disturbing him in a scene of pleasure so truly delicious—so he termed my ruin and shame. After kissing me over and over again, and bestowing various other caresses, he arose and retired through a sliding panel by the bedside, leaving me in the theatre of my undoing overpowered with anguish, more dead than alive. My sufferings, weakness and agitation soon threw me into slumber, in which my ruin and misery were for a time forgotten. Dreadful, indeed, were my sufferings in being deflowered. Never was poor maid so unceremoniously debauched, nor is it possible for anyone to suffer more cruel anguish than I did, in receiving my first lesson from this powerful Turk.

I did not awake from the refreshing sleep I so soundly fell into until late next morning. Upon attempting to rise, I found I was unable, from the dreadful stiffness of the parts that had been so terribly and unmercifully stretched. Unable to rise, I was obliged to remain in the scene of my undoing until the slaves came to awake me. With their assistance I got out of bed. Had you seen the sheets, you would indeed have pitied your poor friend. I found by the care, tenderness and respect with which I was treated that the Dey's orders respecting me must have been very particular.

I learned that he was not expected to return for some time. This news, being unexpected on my part, acted as reprieve would upon a condemned criminal. It, of course, contributed considerably to soothe my wounded feelings; but at the end of a week, just as the flurry of my spirits had in some measure subsided to a degree of composure, I was again thrown into a state of alarm on being informed of his return, as well as his intention to pass that very night with me. I had just retired to bed when the communication was made to me, and his orders were scarcely delivered ere he was in my chamber. The news of his arrival had thrown me into a kind of stupor, from which I did not recover until his fierce kisses brought me to a sense of collection, when I found my second martyrdom was about to commence. You may be assured, from what I have already described of him, that I had nothing to expect from supplication or entreaties; still I did not fail to use them, supported by torrents of tears. These he paid no regard to, but took me in his arms, drawing me to his bosom and calling me foolish and silly to make such opposition to his pleasures. 'Reason a little,' said he, drawing my lips to his, 'consider the indispensable necessity that all loving creatures like yourself are under to lose the sweet flower I so lately gathered from you, which seems to have been so dear to you; consider the great end that nature has created you for, give over these unavailing tears, which only delay your tasting of the sweetest joys. Then you talk about your virtue— pray, can you tell me in what it consists?' cried he, sucking my lips. I could only answer with tears. 'Do you think,' said he, 'if I enjoy you against your will, you are a bit the less virtuous? Or is it possible,' he continued, 'that you are so simple as to believe that virtue depends upon any part of your beautiful body being a little larger or a little less. Of what consideration can it be to Ali whether this part is opened or unopened by man?' and to make me understand the part he meant, he forced his hand between my thighs, where his fiery touches left me in no doubt as to the part he alluded to. He then was proceeding to place me in a situation convenient to satisfy his desires, but because I resisted his attempts, he flew upon me like a tiger, forcibly turned me on my back and divided my thighs; indeed, I found resistance of no avail.

The few days he had been absent seemed to have augmented his desires into a kind of frenzy. I cannot give you anything like a description of my sufferings as he now again forced his dreadful engine into me. The pain I felt was as cruel as when he first deflowered me. The chamber resounded with my shrieks. But he heeded them not; on the contrary, he increased the fury of his thrusts. Three times in the course of a quarter of an hour did I faint in his arms from the dreadful anguish. On recovering I found, during my last insensibility, he had got off me. I cannot tell whether my tears and cries had made any impression on him, or what induced him to get out of bed; but he went to a closet in the room, where I plainly saw him anointing his instrument out of the contents of a small jar. After cleansing his hands, he returned to bed. It was not long ere he again got between my thighs. I lay trembling, expecting the cruel torment; but guess my astonishment when instead of experiencing the thrilling pain which had before always accompanied his penetration I felt him drive it into me up to the very hilt comparatively with no more pain than made me cry out two or three 'Ohs'; but I still felt an extreme tightness accompanied with heated stretching. When I had received him up to the very quick, he tenderly kissed me, and asked if he hurt as much as before. I could not answer such a question, but I believe my blushes must have satisfied him on the point. Indeed, so great was the difference I now felt that I sustained this assault with very little suffering, until nature, unable longer to bear the tumult of pleasure with which the Dey seemed agitated, assisted him, and I for the first time felt with indescribable emotion something warm flowing from him in rapid streams, which deliciously cooled the parts he had so potently warmed. As I felt the last drop ejected from him, he sank on my bosom, without the least sign of animation, stretching himself out to his utmost length, which was the means of drawing his instrument from within me. It hung between my thighs quite bereft of all its power and erection, apparently as lifeless as its owner.

The reason of my escape from his first attack, the night I was brought to the harem, was now sufficiently explained to me. It was not long ere he recovered from his trance. I now perceived a wonderful attention in his behaviour. All his commanding and imperious looks had given way to respectful impassioned regards, although he still did just what he pleased; but there was some change in his manner of acting that I could not in any way account for. Remarkable as I found his attention, it was exceeded by what I soon experienced. Spite of my love for poor Henry, or the repugnance I naturally felt against the Dey as the violator of my chastity—spite of my sufferings in his furious embraces the difference of our religion and ages—can you credit what I felt, even at this early time of my undoing? I blush to write and confess it, but I am obliged to own I felt a voluptuous softness in his kisses, which acted as a balm, soothing me for the pains I had suffered. It is true my lips did not as yet return his pressures, but they submissively received them, inhaling every moment a dissolving poison, which quickly spread through my veins.

By this time I was aware, from the excessive hardness of his instrument, which was now lying on my belly, that it had recovered its wanton life and vigour, and presently the movement of his right hand gave notice I was again about to receive it. But how shall I describe my emotion when, for the first time, I felt it enter me without the smallest particle of pain, with no more difficulty than the mere widening, as he penetrated and stretched each soft furrow, until the whole was completely sheathed and we reached the most complete union without my uttering anything more than a few tremulous sighs—which I could not prevent escaping me in view of the unutterable rapture which the fierce suction created, a sensation which, from being entirely new, was so deliriously indefinable. Do not think me a wanton for thus stating what I experienced. Believe me, I had not the power to resist the soft pleasure he now caused me to taste by the sweet to-and-fro friction of his voluptuous engine.

You, Sylvia, who are yet, I believe, an inexperienced maid, can have no conception of the seductive powers of this wonderful instrument of nature—this terror of virgins, but delight of women. Indeed there can be no description given of the pure delight, I may even say agony of enjoyment, excited by the excessive friction which the rapidity of its thrusts caused. I was soon taught that it was the uncontrolled master key of my feelings. My trembling it quickly banished; my confusion became breathless astonishment, which with the rapidity of lightning changed to a respect for my enjoyer so submissive in its nature that I already looked upon him as the disposer of my future destiny, and my soul became completely and securely resigned to him as he enjoyed my soft body and instructed me in the softest pleasure nature can participate in. My heart, my soul, my very being was melted by his thrilling thrusts, until at last my recollection failed me. I lost sight, and then again sank insensible in his arms, but from a very different cause from my other faintness.

I recovered from this lethargy of pleasure only to be again thrown into the same dissolving state, for the Dey, charmed with my entire submission, seemed determined that nothing should be wanting on his part to make my bliss complete. Being entirely relieved of pain, I swam in the sea of thrilling delight and enjoyment only known to the young maids just released from the pangs of expiring virginity. With these all my pains and fears vanished, together with the remains of my virgin bashfulness, the only thing that could throw any obstacle in the way of this luxurious novelty which so ravishingly filled my soul with ecstasy and astonishment. Although I yet had scarcely summed up courage to look my enjoyer in the face, the warmth of my caresses and tenderness of my kisses, the voluptuous agitation of my whole body, all sufficiently satisfied him how firmly the pleasure had fixed its seductive influence on my senses; and in the midst of our enjoyment, at the very moment he had worked my feelings into a state of delirium indescribable, he suddenly stopped his ravishing, luxurious movements, and kissing me with a softness that rushed thrilling to my heart, said, 'Lovely houri, will you pardon me for the little respect I paid you in teaching you the mysteries of love?' Nearly fainting with the joy I possessed, I languishingly, for the first time, ventured to lift my eyes full in the face of my seducer but, unable to bear the brilliant luster of his eyes, I hid my blushes in his bosom, where he felt his pardon sealed by a burning kiss. This unequivocal and tender acknowledgement of his power over me rekindled all his nearly satisfied desires, and, drawing my lips to his with a gust of passion time can never obliterate the remembrance of, he made me feel him in a manner so exquisitely touching, by such lovely and timely degrees, that I blessed the happy chance that had thrown me into his powerful arms.

In this manner was a great part of the night spent, until exhausted nature requiring a truce to our conflicts, we unconsciously fell asleep in each other's arms. In the morning I awoke first; the Dey was tying on his back, with one of his arms under his head, the other by his side. There was not the slightest particle of bedclothes on either of us. In my sleep the pillow had got from under my head; on raising myself to replace it, I caught a glimpse of that terrible machine which had so furiously agitated me with pain and pleasure. I assure you, Sylvia, I could not look at it without considerable remains of terror, but my alarm was strongly mixed up with feelings of tenderness and respect I thought my eyes would now be satisfied with inspecting it, but was much disappointed with its present appearance. It hung over his thigh shrunk up into a small size, seemingly perfectly incapable of exciting the various sensations I had so potently felt However, reduced as it was in appearance, it had the same power of fascination over me which is attributed to the serpent's eye over the bird. I could not withdraw mine from it, and so intense was my survey that I did not observe the Dey had awoke, and was enjoying my abstraction of mind.

His laughing at me broke the spell which the sight I was engaged in had worked round my senses. To be caught in this occupation, you may be sure, threw me into infinite confusion; every part of me was covered with blushes, which I strived to hide in the bedclothes; but he took me in his arms, still laughing, covering me with kisses, and told me I had seen everything at a great disadvantage, but I should presently be gratified by a view which would please me. This kind of discourse, instead of diminishing, added to my confusion. But, to crown all, he seized my right hand, and, with gentle compulsion, forced into it what may be termed nature's grand masterpiece. I faintly struggled as I received it, but he was determined I should observe the effect of my hand on his sensible part. At first it was as soft as a piece of sponge, but immediately it felt the warmth of my pressure, it began to throb, then to expand, and in a few moments that which at first I held with ease became a column of ivory, which I declare I could not even grasp. As he drew my hand up and down, it every moment seemed to increase in strength and length, until it attained so magnificent an erection that I could scarcely credit my sight. Is it possible, said I to myself, that so tremendous a pillar could have been buried within me? My other hand, governed by my thoughts, strayed between my thighs to examine the possibility of my entertaining such a guest. This movement of my hand in an instant discovered my thoughts to the Dey, 'What,' said he, drawing me to his bosom, 'do you doubt the possibility? Come, come, I shall soon remove your doubts; besides it is just you should reap the crop your hand has raised. Saying this, he softly turned me on my back, and got between my thighs, which I now willingly extended to receive him. Seeing my hair was in considerable confusion from our overnight's conflict, he leisurely placed it in order, laying the curls on my neck and breasts in the manner he thought most tempting. Having finished this employment, with his right hand he seized my left and, forcing it between his thighs, told me to pilot the vessel, as: he called it, safe into port. You may guess how completely he had subdued and mastered my feelings when I tell you, Sylvia, that I instantly obeyed his directions. When he felt I had lodged it between the lips, he withdrew my hand, and I quickly felt the fierce insertion up to the quick. The narrowness was now no more than what heightened the pleasure of the Dey in the strict embraces of that tender, warm sheath round the instrument that had made it fit for that which it was so luxuriously adapted. After three or four thrusts, which he made, as it were, to satisfy me as to its being entirely engulfed, he directed me to place my legs over his back. I instantly did as he requested. As a reward for my compliance, he drew out his shaft, all but the head, then drove it home into me eight or nine times in rapid succession, until I was stirred beyond bearing by the furious agitation it caused within me. I lay gasping, gorged and crammed to suffocation with rapture, till his short breathings, faltering accents, eyes twinkling with humid fires, and lunges more furious with increased stiffness gave me full notice of the approach of the dissolving period. It came—he died away on my bosom, distilling a flood within me that shot into the innermost recesses of my body, every conduit of which was upon the flow to meet and voluptuously to mix with his melting essence. As our mutual juices met and became one fluid, I sank insensible, drowned in a sea of delight of which words can convey no description.

Thus passed the second night of my undoing. After he had left me in the morning, and reason had resumed its empire, I was fully sensible of my deviation from strict virtue in the return I had made to his pleasure. This for a time filled my mind with melancholy thoughts, but I reflected it was the will of Heaven that my virginity should be reserved for the Dey. It was a thing settled by fate, that he should possess it, and I soon became entirely resigned, ceasing to reproach myself about that which I had no control over. The next day I was introduced to three of his other ladies—one French, one Italian, and one Greek. They were all lovely. The Grecian is named Zena, and I think I never beheld anything so lovely. She appeared about seventeen years of age, fair as a lily, with all the charms and freshness of her age, whilst the modest languish of her fine dark eyes, combined with a settled melancholy, gave an interesting appearance to her countenance which made her look peculiarly attractive. I felt great interest in this young girl, and will give you an outline of her history, and also that of the French and Italian ladies. I shall begin with the Italian, who spoke French equally as well as the Frenchwoman herself, and who related to me the short history of her coming into the possession of the Dey. I shall relate just as she repeated it to me. She was a most lovely woman, gracefully formed, with fine black languishing eyes, capable of creating the greatest interest; but she appeared of delicate health; her voice was tender, her mouth was rather large, but her admirably made lips with regular teeth, quite hid the defect; so fine and beautiful a head of hair I think I never saw; in fact, her person altogether was sufficient to create desire in the bosom of age itself. She related her story in nearly the following words:

'The city of Genoa, where I was born, has been always famed above any town in Europe for the refinement of its gallantry. It is common there for a gentleman to profess himself the humble servant of a handsome woman and to wait upon her to serve in every public place for twenty years together without ever seeing her in private or being entitled to any greater favour than a kind look or a touch of her fair hand. Of all this sighing tribe, the most constant, and the most respectful of all those I knew was Signer Ludovico, my lover. My name is Honoria Grimaldi, I am the only daughter of a senator of that name, and I was esteemed a very great beauty in Genoa, but at the same time quite a prude, and most reserved.' The remark made me laugh, for she had the look of a very great libertine. 'You may smile, but so great was nicety then, in point of love, that although I could not be insensible to the address of Signer Ludovico, yet I could not bring myself to think of marrying my lover, which would have admitted him to freedoms which I thought entirely inconsistent with true modesty—freedoms which then, I assure you, made me shudder to think of.'

I here asked whether the Dey had not rectified her ideas on that point. She blushed and sighed, 'Indeed, Madame, he was not long in effecting that change of opinion. In vain, Madame, did Ludovico speak of the violence of his passion for me. I answered that mine for him was no less so. But it was his mind I loved; I enjoyed that without having to go to bed with him, the very thought of which shocked and alarmed me. My lover was ready to despair at these discourses; he could not but admire such fine sentiments, yet he wished I had not been so perfect. He wrote me a long, melancholy letter. I returned him one for answer in verses, full of sublime expressions about my love, but not a word that tended to satisfy the poor man's impatience. At last he applied himself to my father, and to engage him to use his authority, offered to take me without a portion. My father, who was a plain man, was mighty pleased with this proposal, and made no difficulty to promise him success. Accordingly he very roughly told me that I must be married the next day or go to a nunnery. This dilemma startled me very much. In spite of all my repugnance to the marriage bed, I found something about me extremely averse to a cloister. An absolute separation from Ludovico was what I could not bear; it was even worse than absolute conjunction. In this distress, not knowing what to do, I turned over about a hundred romances in search for precedents. After many struggles with myself, I resolved to surrender upon terms; therefore, I told my lover I consented to be his wife, provided I might be so by degrees, and that after the ceremony was over he should not pretend at once to all the rights and privileges of a husband, but allow my modesty to make a decent and gradual surrender. Ludovico did not much like such a capitulation, but rather than not have me, he was content to pay the last compliment to my delicacy. We were united, and at the end of the first month he was happy to find himself arrived at full enjoyment of my lips.


'Whilst he was thus gaining ground, inch by inch, his father died, and left him a large estate in Corsica. His presence was necessary there, but he could not think of parting with me, so we embarked together, and Ludovico had good hopes that he should not take possession of his estate only, but of my virginity too, at his arrival. Whether it was that Venus, who is said to have been born out of the sea, was more powerful mere than on land, or whether it was from the freedom that is usual on board a ship, but whatever the reason it is sure that during the voyage I indulged him in greater liberties than he ever presumed to take before, for my neck and breasts were moulded by his bold hand. But while he was thus by degrees, as it were, reducing me to his wishes, fortune, who took a pleasure in persecuting him, brought an African corsair in our way, who quickly put an end to our dalliance by making us both slaves. Who can express our affliction and despair at so sudden and ill-timed a captivity? Ludovico saw himself bereft of his virgin bride on the very point of obtaining all his wishes, and I had reason to apprehend from the rough hands I had fallen into that my virginity was likely to be taken from me, whether I resisted or not. But the martyrdom I looked for on the instant was unexpectedly deferred, for the corsair, seeing I was handsome, thought me worthy of the embraces of the Dey, and to him I was presented on our arrival here—unfortunate end to all my pure and heroic sentiments! The time was now arrived when I was doomed to be courted in a manner opposite to that adopted by Ludovico. My being a married woman was known to my captor, and was a fact which, of course, he communicated to the Dey. He naturally supposed me to be a finished woman. When I was brought to him he appeared much struck with my appearance, and instantly ordered everyone out of the apartment; then, rising off the couch he was sitting on, he took my hand and led me towards it. On approaching it to my great astonishment he desired me in good Italian to be seated. I obeyed trembling, and he seated himself by my side. Directly he had seated himself he took hold of one of my hands, and demanded from what part of Italy I came. From the mildness of his speech and manner, I thought I could assume the same authority with him as I had done with Ludovico, so would scarcely answer any of his questions, whereupon the Dey, seeing the more tender and respectful his behaviour was, the more I presumed on his forbearance, suddenly seized me round the waist, and drawing my lips forcibly to his, continued sucking them with such force that he nearly made me faint. The suddenness of the attack threw me into extreme confusion. Ere I recovered from it, the Dey had uncovered my breasts and was handling them just as he pleased, exclaiming every moment, as he pressed and handled them, "By Mahomet, how deliciously formed they are! How firm! How delightfully the nipples pout!" and such-like observations, which covered me with burning blushes.

'By this time I had recovered somewhat from my confusion, observing which the Dey, rising from the coach, said, in a low, determined tone, "How now, audacious slave, do you presume to oppose the will of thy master? Show again the least opposition to my desires and in an instant I shall have thee scourged properly for thy presumption. So mark me, slave!" After this menace he again seated himself and drew me upon his knees, with his arms round my waist. His determined manner of treating me had such an effect that I dared not resist his forcing his hand again into my breasts; but after he had sufficiently satisfied himself with feeling and moulding them, he suddenly turned his hands under my petticoats. His threats were now forgotten; I again strenuously resisted and struggled, whereupon he immediately desisted, and getting off the couch, with a small whistle which hung on his belt, he called in his black eunuchs, to one of whom he gave some orders in the Turkish language; the fellow went out, but quickly returned with a whip, which had about a dozen tails. I was now seized by the two eunuchs, who forced me across the couch with my face downwards; each of the eunuchs held me over the couch by the arm, so that I could not possibly get away. Having me thus secure and unmindful of my tears or entreaties, the Dey lifted up my clothes, and threw them all over my shoulders, leaving everything below my waist as naked as when I was born. Would you believe it, Madame, he began to flog me in so unmerciful a manner that I could not retain my screams, of which he took not the least

notice until he thought he had sufficiently punished my first offence. He then left off, and demanded if I would dare to oppose
his wishes again. I could not at the moment have answered him,
even if death had been the consequence. However, he allowed
me very little time, but recommenced his flogging again, saying, "Oh, you are sullen are you? But I shall soon subdue you."
Indeed, so painfully did I feel his lashes that at last I was able to
cry that I would be submissive to his desires.


'I was directly relieved from the position I was in, and
the eunuchs were dismissed, when the Dey, just as if nothing
had happened, placed himself by my side; but, seeing I sat extremely uneasily from the soreness of the part he had so unmercifully whipped, he caused me to lie down on my side, laying
himself beside me. He then drew me to his bosom and after
kissing away my tears, sucking my lips and forcing his tongue
into my mouth (which created great disgust in me), presently
demanded if I was not married, I shuddered out an affirmative.
"Curses on the Christian dog, I say, that has plucked your virginity!" he replied; "by Ali, I would have possessed it." You
may be sure, Madame, this made me blush, which made him
remark how much my blushes increased my beauty. Again my
lips became his prey. "How long have you been joined to the
Christian dog?" demanded he, withdrawing his lips to let me
answer him. I stammered out, "Only a month." "A month have
thy blushes, then, been polluted. Well, I must be content with
you as you are. Indeed, you are a feast fit for a monarch. How
languishingly delicious is the modest cast of your eyes! Kiss
me, trembler!" I dared not disobey, and, covered with blushes,
joined my lips to his. He seemed much pleased with my obedience, and continued for some time most passionately kissing
me. Whilst thus occupied, he slipped his right hand again under
my petticoats and shift. A dreadful trembling seized me, but
my fears prevented the least resistance, whilst his burning hand

travelled over my most secret charms. Here was a change, Madame, from the respect of poor Ludovico! The smallest favour was not granted to him until after the most urgent persuasions, whilst the Dey took every liberty he thought fit, and I believe thought he was conferring an honour upon me. He had now got his hand between my thighs and, drawing my lips closer to his, he desired me to open them a little wider, that he might have full command of the shrine of pleasure where he said he meant presently to sacrifice. I did not at the moment obey him. "How now," he cried, changing his tone from the soliciting to the commanding, "Darest thou neglect my orders?" Oh, Madame, the gradual extension of my thighs plainly spoke my fears. My tears flowed in torrents; my breasts heaved in convulsive agony. For a moment or so the Dey played with the soft down that crowns the mount of pleasure, and then slipped his finger between the lips of the road which until then had never been travelled, little dreaming of the discovery he was about to make. Indeed, on forcing his finger as far as he could into me, with great astonishment he found some difficulty in effecting entry, his efforts making me cry out that he hurt me. Surprised at my cries, he instantly started up, and forcing me on my back, extended my thighs to their utmost width, "Why, by Mahomet, you are a maid!" he cried, as he minutely examined me. "What punishment do you think you deserve for thus deceiving me as to your virginity?" Trembling and panting with shame and fear, I replied that I had not deceived him, as he had only asked how long I had been married, and I had told him the truth. "Then how is it," he demanded, "that your husband has not reaped his rights?" I at last confessed my maiden bashfulness had been the reason. At this the Dey laughed heartily, saying, "Whatever is the cause, holy Mahomet, I thank you for this unexpected treasure, but it shall not hang long on the stock for want of plucking." He then got off the couch, also assisting me to rise off my back; then applying the whistle to his mouth he summoned the same eunuchs, to whom he gave some directions as before. In obedience to his instructions they conducted me into a small room, every side of which was covered with glass: even the door at which I entered I could not discover when shut. In the centre of the room was a low dark-cushioned velvet couch, with one large cushion at the head; it was nothing but a plain broad couch, in the centre of which was fastened, properly extended, a beautiful white damask cloth.

'I was stripped in an instant by the eunuchs of every particle of my dress; they even untied the fillets which fastened up my hair; then, having reduced me to a complete state of nature, they retired, taking away my clothes. So much were my feelings overcome, that I was obliged to seat myself on the couch, or else I must have fallen. I was not doomed to wait long in suspense, for in a few seconds the Dey entered, as naked as myself. You, Madame, no doubt well know how little ceremony, in cases of this kind, he uses. He took me in his arms, after kissing me, and told me he was now come to redress the wrongs I had suffered in the cruel neglect of my husband. "But," he said, "it will soon be repaired; you quickly shall taste such joys as your beauties so well deserve you should partake of. But why these tears and sighs? Is this the way you meet my caresses and kindness? Is this the return you make my generosity in preparing to teach you those pleasure which your husband has neglected. Come, come, let me have no more of this folly!" So drawing me to his bosom, he gently forced me on my back. "There now," he said, "lie down—no, not that way," seeing I was placing myself on my side, "it is on your back you must receive your first instructions. There, that's right; now open your soft thighs!" In an instant he was between them. I found I could not dare disobey. Finding my thighs were not quite extended enough, he soon widened them to his wish. I need not tell you how tremendously large the Dey is; turn in which way I would I could not help seeing in the glass the terrible pillar with which he was preparing to skewer me; quickly discovering the cause of my exces-

sive alarm, whilst he was fixing its head between the lips of my virgin sheath, he tried by every kind of endearment to soothe me, assuring me the pain would be nothing—that my fears were unfounded; besides it was a sacrifice which nature had decreed, and once over the sweetest joys would be my reward; then why these foolish fears? Thus did he soften me to his desires. The head of his instrument was no sooner fixed in the opening than by four or five sudden shoves he contrived to insert the whole of it entirely, so that I could not see any part of it as my face turned towards the glass. At this moment his penetration was not deep enough to make me experience any great pain, but he, well knowing what was coming, forcibly secured one of his arms around my body.

'Everything was now prepared and favourable. My legs were glued to his, and I lay in his arms as it were insensible from despair, shame and confusion. He now began to improve his advantage by forcibly deepening his penetration; his prodigious stiffness and size gave me such dreadful anguish, from the separation of the sides of the soft passage by such a hard substance, that I could not refrain from screaming. Delicate as I was, he found great difficulty; but his Herculean strength in the end broke down all my virgin defenses. My piercing cries spoke of my sufferings. In my agony I strove to escape, but the Dey, perfectly used to such attempts, easily foiled them by his able thrusts, and quickly buried his tremendous instrument too far within me to leave me any chance of escape. He now paid no kind of attention to my sufferings, but followed up his movements with fury, until the tender texture altogether gave way to his fierce tearing and rending, and one merciless, violent thrust broke in and carried all before it, sending his weapon, imbued and reeking with the blood of my virginity, up to its utmost length in my body. The piercing shriek I gave proclaimed that I felt it up to the very quick; in short, his victory was complete.

'What my sufferings at first were I need not dwell upon, as no doubt you must have experienced them as painfully as myself, from his extraordinary size. It was also increased from the want of delicacy he used in subduing me. But my suffering did not seem to be any consideration with him, for he gave me no respite in his proceedings, but by enjoyment after enjoyment very soon blunted the sharpness of the pain, and ere he withdrew from me I had sustained four assaults, which from their amorous fury had so stretched and opened me as to ensure I need never again complain on the score of suffering. Being satisfied on this point, he withdrew his shaft, and laying himself for a short time by my side, covered every part of me with burning kisses and caresses, assuring me that my sufferings were ended, and that I should shortly enjoy the pleasure of unmixed and pure delight in a manner that would reward me for all the anguish I had experienced in his fierce embraces. After reposing a short time on my bosom he got up and assisted me off the couch, which bore crimson evidence of my late loss. "Look," he cried, "my sweet slave," fondly pressing me in his arms, "I shall have your name worked in letters of gold on it, and it will then be deposited with a number of others that ornament a room in my harem. By virtue of this you are entitled to many privileges, which will be explained to you. Among others you are forever exempt from any kind of attendance on my wives or chief sultanas, unless you choose to amuse yourself. But the slaves who will attend you will explain all the things which the blushing testimony of your chastity entitles you to." He then placed such a thrilling kiss on my lips that it threw me into the greatest confusion.

'He now called some Turkish slaves, who brought every kind of female clothing. They were not long in completing my toilet. This finished, he conducted me into a magnificent room, where refreshments were laid out during the repast the Dey, by the most assiduous attention, strove to render himself agreeable, but as yet I could scarcely venture to look on him. It was still early in the morning. When we had finished our repast, he tenderly enquired if I felt inclined to refresh myself by taking some repose alone. He could not have proposed anything more agreeable, which must have been evident by the immediate assent I gave to his offer. I was directly supported by him to a sleeping apartment, where, after again and again tenderly kissing me, he left me with a female slave, who soon undressed me; and in a soft slumber, which I soon fell into, my misfortunes were forgotten. My sleep was long and of course refreshing. I was awoken by the slave, who informed me that dinner was nearly ready, I got up and was assisted by her to dress. I then took dinner. After dinner the slave drew my attention to a large quantity of books, in my own language, which the Dey had caused to be sent to me. I found them to consist of our choicest authors. In my sitting-room he had occasioned a grand pianoforte to be placed, also an excellent lute, with a quantity of music, that I might not want amusement. I soon found several large portfolios of all kinds of prints, which alone were an inexhaustible store of amusement. The time imperceptibly passed in inspecting the various things which were placed for my recreation, until the slave reminded me that it was time I retired, as it was the Dey's intention to pass the night with me. What could I do? Resistance was now out of the question; my virtue and modesty had received their mortal wounds. I had, even if I wished, no resource; indeed, nothing was left to me but to submit to my fate. Scarcely knowing where I was going, I was conducted to the bedchamber, and soon was reduced to a proper state to meet the Dey's desires, being placed in bed in a state of panting, blushing confusion, very little different from that state I was in in the morning, when he debauched me. I was not long kept in suspense. I soon found myself in his strong arms. But, oh, how changed I now found him! All the authority of a master which he had so strongly assumed in the morning was now lost in the most passionate and tender regards of a most devoted and even submissive lover—even poor Ludovico could not be more so. I soon found his present proceedings more fatal to my morality than all the favours he had ravished from me by force under the influence of punishment. Indeed, I cannot explain the feeling he soon created. As I lay on his bosom he kissed me in a manner quite new, keeping my mouth to his several minutes, every now and then thrusting in his tongue and sucking mine. All the time he was doing this his hand was travelling over every part of my body with burning touches, creating the greatest disorder. The unopposed enjoyment of my lips, and feeling every secret beauty I possessed had now so heated his spirits, that to prevent the fluid that was boiling within him being improperly lost, it was absolutely necessary there should be no delay in my resigning to him the possession of the gates of pleasure. So for had his pressures and touches heated and inflamed me, that he found no obstacle in turning me on my back and again placing himself between my extended thighs. I scarcely recollect how it was, but I certainly felt at the moment he was fixing his instrument the soft prelude of pleasure illuminating within me. From trembling and fear I already began to desire; and, good God! How can I describe the surprise I felt when with one energetic shove he lodged himself up to the hilt in me without the smallest sensation of pain. Never, oh never shall I forget the delicious transports that followed the stiff insertion; and then, ah me! By what thrilling degrees did he, by his luxurious movements, fiery kisses, and strange touches of his hand in the most private parts of my body, reduce me to a voluptuous state of insensibility. I blush to say so powerfully did his ravishing instrument stir up nature within me, that by mere instinct I returned him kiss for kiss, responsively meeting his fierce thrusts, until the fury of the pleasure and ravishment became so overpowering that, unable longer to support the excitement I so luxuriously felt, I fainted in his arms with pleasure, Ludovico, the flogging, and everything else was entirely driven out of my head. So lively, so repeated were the enjoyments that the Dey caused me to participate in with him, I wondered how nature could have slumbered so long within me. I was lost in astonishment that in all the caresses I received from Ludovico he had not contrived to give the slightest alarm or feeling to nature. I could not help smiling at my ignorance when I considered the ridiculous airs I had assumed to Ludovico about my chastity. The Dey, indeed, had soon discovered my folly, and like a man of sense, took the proper method to subdue me. In this way, in one short night, you see, he put to the rout all my pure modest virgin scruples, rapturously teaching me the nature of love's sacred mysteries, and the great end for which we poor weak females are created.

'During the first month of my captivity, my senses were kept in such a continual flow of rapture that what with sustaining his embraces at night and refreshing myself with sleep during the day, I had little else to do. But by degrees his visits to my apartment became less and less frequent, from the numerous beauties that came into his possession it could not be otherwise, but when I am honoured with embraces, so tender, so kind are his caresses, that I feel sufficiently repaid for his long absence, although I cannot but wish his visits were more frequent. But I am content with my lot. I have now been in the harem nearly two years. This is my short history. Of Ludovico I have never heard anything since we parted, and under all circumstances I think it as well I should not, for it would now be impossible for me to return to him with anything like satisfaction to myself, so firmly has the Dey fixed himself in my affections.'

I have now, dear Sylvia, given you the history of the Italian beauty. I must confess the latter part of her history, which related to the gradual decrease of the Dey's visits, gave me a very uncomfortable sensation at first; but I was afterwards angry with myself for entertaining it a moment, when I considered during the whole time I have been in his possession, three nights out of every week have as yet been spent in his arms. Nor have I observed the least relaxation in either his attentions or desires. But I have been most dreadfully alarmed by something this Italian has communicated, which at first I did not give the least credit to. When we had related to each other our histories, of course we became considerably more intimate and familiar in our conversation. She asked me whether I felt any pleasure when the Dey enjoyed me behind. I told her I did not understand what she meant by behind. She laughed most immoderately at my ignorance, and would scarcely credit what I had asserted, particularly as she knew the Dey was so fond of the other route. I requested her to explain herself. 'Are you not aware,' said she, 'that a woman has two maidenheads to take?' On my replying in the negative, she answered, 'You have, though. Under the altar of Venus is another grotto, a little more obscure, to be sure; but there the Dey will offer up his sacrifices with characteristic energy.' I was all in a tremble at this discourse, and demanded of her if the Dey had ever enjoyed her in that position. 'Most certainly, many times,' was her reply. 'If you doubt what I say, the next time I am favoured with a morning visit by the Dey, you shall judge with your own eyes as to the fact; it can be easily managed, as our suites of rooms are contiguous.'

'Is it possible,' cried I, 'that you receive any pleasure from a conjunction so beastly and unnatural?'

'What innocence, my dear, what childishness!' replied the libertine. 'Do you not know that the men consider every part of us formed entirely for their pleasures; one enjoys us one way, one another, each man according to his lechery. You may rely upon it one of these days the Dey will instruct you in this way and rectify your ideas on the subject.'

This conversation, and other matters which this Italian informed me of and which I could not drive from my thoughts, threw a considerable gloom over my feelings. In the evening the Dey visited me, and immediately saw by my countenance that something had disordered me. After considerable persuasion he contrived to extract what had caused my distress.

'And why should this, dearest Zulima, give you any uneasiness?' said he, tenderly taking me in his arms and kissing me. 'I can see no reason why it should have raised a cloud on this lovely face; nor could I for a moment have supposed, if I had requested my sweet slave to have administered to my joys in that way, there would have been any denial. I hid my face in his bosom, and told him in our country it was considered the most degrading crime that could be committed, that it was punished with death.

'I am aware,' replied he, 'that the English nation consider it a crime, but I was not acquainted with the magnitude of the punishment. But, Zulima' (I forgot to mention before that I received a new name from the Dey, as is customary with all captives), 'your country is the only one in the world that either considers it a crime or punishes it. Besides, Zulima, you are not in England now, nor are you likely ever to go there again. You are mine until one of us shall shake off this mortal form; therefore, you must submit to everything that I conceive will be an addition to my pleasures. Does not the English law direct that the wife shall be obedient to the husband in all lawful desires?'

'Yes,' I replied.


'Well, then, although you are not my wife in fact, still you are, according to our laws, considered the same. To become my married wife you must change your religion. But still you are considered my wife, therefore must submit to my lawful desires. By our laws we are permitted to enjoy our wives or concubines in any way that adds to our luxuries; in other words it is lawful that I may enjoy, and you must resign your second virginity whenever I require you to do so. After all, dear Zulima, how can it possibly be construed into a crime? It is true that the seed which I have so often distilled within you with such dissolving pleasure is given by nature to multiply our species, so to divert its natural course may in some measure be construed as an offence against nature by those who do not give it any consideration. Put the case thus: to divert and cast away seed is a crime. Now it is clear that the seed, even when deposited in its natural receiver, is entirely lost forty-nine times out of fifty. For instance, immediately sufficient seed is injected into the womb, the female conceives; then the mouth of the womb closes, and until the delivery of the child does not open again. If the female is fruitful, and properly enjoyed, she will conceive to a certainty in three months; it is six months more at least ere she will be delivered of her burden; consequently at every embrace the female sustains after conception, the seed that is shot within her is entirely lost or misused. Now what difference can there be as to where the seed is lost if it be lost? Where is the offence or crime? What difference whether the seed is uselessly deposited in the grotto of Venus, or injected in the temple below it? None in the world, lovely slave! My Grecian and Corsican slaves submit to any kind of enjoyment as a matter of duty and submission, in which they are instructed from their infancy. I have two Italians who think it no kind of crime; to my French slave it is a mere bagatelle. I was aware of the prejudices of your nation, and from the joys I found in your embraces did not like even to broach the subject to you.'

'Then,' cried I, throwing my arms round his neck and fondly kissing him, 'let the pleasures you confess I have afforded you save me from what I consider would be the greatest disgrace I could possibly experience.'

'This is folly,' cried the Dey, 'I can make no promise of the kind.'

'But you must,' I replied.

'How?' demanded he. 'You have sworn by your holy Prophet to grant me any favour I choose to request; you recollect your sacred oath?'

'I do certainly.'

'Well, then, the favour I request is that I may be spared the pollution we have been discoursing of.'

'Can Zulima think that any act of Ali would pollute her?' cried he, rising from the couch with great heat and indignation. It was the first unkind word he had used to me since he had me. My heart sank within me whilst he continued, 'It is true I made the oath, and must religiously observe it. I shall leave you to reflect, foolish slave, on your childishness in thus attempting to bind my pleasures by an oath made in a moment when your deceitful blandishments had softened me into a belief that your love and devotion to me was as sincere as your person is beautiful. When you have altered your opinion you can inform the chief eunuch. I may, perhaps, then pardon this insult, and restore you to favour.' He then left me, muttering the word 'pollution', unmindful of my tears, which quickly began to flow at his angry looks.

As he went out of the room my spirits failed me entirely. I sank on the couch overwhelmed with grief, railing against the mischance that brought me acquaintance with this Italian, whom I considered as the cause of my rupture with the Dey. My tears continued for nearly an hour after his departure, which no doubt considerably relieved me. However, I began to comfort myself with the hopes that his anger would not last. But, indeed, I did not properly estimate his character. The next day passed without my seeing him; a second, third, fourth passed in anxious, I may say almost breathless anguish, watching and listening for the approach of his well-known footstep. Guess the cruel suspense I suffered. Habituated to the sweet pleasure of his embraces, my desires began rapidly to overpower the scruples which early precept had instilled in me. My unsatisfied feelings became every hour stronger and stronger, until on the fifth day I was again visited by Honoria, the Italian, who entertained me with a long account of her happiness, having passed two nights running with the Dey; her transports went like daggers to my heart, but gave the decisive turn to my wavering indecision. I instantly resolved to submit to the Dey's desires, and wrote him a letter accordingly.

# Letter 5

Emily to the Dey


Oh, Ali, is it possible that you, who have so often sworn that it made you unhappy to be for a day absent from your Zulima, can it be believed that for a whole week you would thus desert her? Your cruelty makes me suffer more than words can speak. You know I had no intention to give offence in what I uttered at our last interview. How could you leave me in the way you did? Oh, Ali, I am with child; hasten to comfort your miserable slave. You cannot doubt my love. Since the day you overpowered my innocence (the day I consider the happiest of my existence, although truly it was a painful one), how many proofs have you received of my love and devotion? Hasten then to do me justice, I conjure you. Surely I need not remind you of what I lost in becoming yours—my native country, innumerable friends, virtue. Oh, Ali, do not longer punish me; I am all devotion to your every desire, your submissive slave,


ZULIMA

# Letter 6

Ali to his slave Zulima

I have received your letter. I was aware of your being with child. Were it possible to increase my love for you this would be the cause, but lovely as you are, and dote upon you as I do, I am determined to tear myself from your tempting arms until I find your submission perfect. You write about your loss of virtue, country and friends by falling into my power. Recollect the pleasure I have taught you and caused you to experience-have they not sufficiently rewarded you for the virginity you brought me? You say you are all devotion and submission to my every desire-be more explicit. Have you made up your mind to absolve me from my oath? Mark me! Never more will these arms enfold you until by resigning your second maidenhead I have put it out of your power to dispute with me on this point. Write to me more explicitly—say you meant to absolve and submit to my embraces in the way I wish, and then you will meet with a return of my most ardent affection.

ALI

My veins were on fire -I could deny him nothing, and wrote the following note:

# Letter 7

Emily to the Dey


I submit—I absolve you from your oath—fly to the arms of your longing


ZULIMA


Directly he was assured of my wish to absolve him of his oath, he appointed the same day to receive the last proof of my entire submission. In the evening when he entered my chamber I could not help flying to his arms. Unconsciously my eyes were filled with tears; but I did not consider them tears of sorrow, but rather of the pleasure I felt at feeling myself pressed in his arms again. He gave me a long and thrilling kiss, but seeing I was about to reproach him for his neglect, he stopped my mouth by informing me that he could not have his joys dampened by any silly upbraidings, but should instantly proceed, to prevent a repetition of our quarrel, by at once removing its cause; and he began immediately to undress me, which from the nature of my Turkish attire was soon accomplished. From the ardent caresses he placed upon my neck and breasts, and indeed every other part that became exposed, I felt assured the power of my attractions had not diminished. When he had stripped me naked he disrobed himself, then taking me in his arms, placed me on the couch, my stomach underneath, on two round pillows, one of them coming against the lower part of my belly, so as to elevate my bottom considerably.

Having placed me thus, he divided my thighs to their utmost extension, leaving the route he intended to penetrate fairly open to his attack. He now got upon me, and having, as he thought, placed himself securely, he encircled my body round my loins with both his arms, and strove to penetrate the obstacle nature had placed in his way; but so largely is he proportioned that his efforts were at first without effect. Again he attempted, but again failed, and making a desperate lunge, his arrow, instead of piercing where he intended it should, slipped into the shrine of Venus, and before he found out his mistake, to my inexpressible delight it was nearly buried in its proper sanctuary. But he was not to be foiled in that way; he instantly withdrew it and again fixing its head proceeded with great caution and fierceness; in short, he soon got the head entirely fixed. His efforts then became more and more energetic. But he was as happy as the satisfying of his beastly will could make him. He regarded me not, but profiting by his success, soon completed my second undoing; and then, indeed, with mingled emotions of disgust and pain, I sensibly felt the debasement of being the slave of a luxurious Turk.

I was now, indeed, wretched and oppressed with mental anguish, until at last my outraged feeling could no longer sustain the shock. A delirious fever seized me. Bereft of my senses, I know not what further took place at that time. The Dey has since informed me that a considerable time elapsed ere he found out my loss of reason, but immediately he ascertained the state I was in, he was compelled to desist by his religion, for it is sacrilege to touch or injure any person, Turk or Christian, who is deranged. Every advice and medical assistance were immediately procured to restore my senses, which was soon effected; and when my health was again sufficiently reestablished to enable me to receive his visits, again was I compelled in silence to resign myself to his infamous desires, until by repeated en-

gagements I became accustomed to his proceedings. But the only result is, if anything, an augmentation of my disgust and horror. By my submission I was reinstated in his affections, and everything proceeds as usual. But the charm is broken. It is true he can, when he pleases, bewilder my senses in the softest confusion; but when the tumult is over, and my blood cooled from the fermentation he causes-when reason resumes its sway, I feel that the silken cords of affection which bound me so securely to him have been so much loosened that he will never again be able to draw them together so closely as they were before he subdued me to his abominable desires.

My depression of spirits made me quite the laughing stock of the Italian woman and the French woman, who were perfectly acquainted with the cause. They affected to despise my feelings. The only consolation I received was from the Grecian girl, with whom I had become extremely intimate and to whom I was much attached. She was a beautiful girl, tall and slender; her face was rather pale and languid, overcast with a melancholy resignation, but her light-blue eyes were mild and expressive as the soft ray of an autumnal moon tingeing a fading evening sky. With the help of books I had been able to teach her the English language, and her progress in attaining it was almost incredible. We could now converse freely together, and mourn over our misfortunes and captivity. I shall narrate her distressing history in nearly the same words as she stated it to me.

### History of Adianti the Grecian Slave

My name is Adianti. I was born in the delightful island of Macaria, where my father was a merchant, called Theodoricus. I am his only child. Like all Greeks or Christians who reside under the power of Turks, my father was obliged to live in a style of the utmost simplicity. It was only by stealth he ventured on any little luxurious indulgence, well knowing that the governor of the district was upon the watch to pounce upon him the moment he made a show of property. Slavery, the most powerful agent in the degradation of mankind, has given to the modern Greeks a melancholy propensity to indulge in all kinds of gloomy presages and forebodings. I was not exempt from the feelings of my countrymen, and my very name, being that of one of the Danaides, whenever I heard it mentioned, always carried an ominous feeling to my heart.

In our neighbourhood resided a youth named Demetrius, the only son of an aged and infirm widow. He was born for a land of freedom, and one might have predicted from his appearance that he was destined to chafe and struggle not a little under the restraints and mortifications which ever fall to the lot of those who show the least spirit of independence. His stature was tall; he carried his head higher than a Bashaw; he was of easy carriage, and his body as straight as a palm; active and graceful in his walk, clear in his eye, and impatient of insult to the last degree. He was eloquent, poetical, romantic, enterprising and a lover of the arts—he could have achieved great things had his lot been cast in a more happy age and country. Were he now living he would be foremost among the heroes who are defending our religion.

An ancient intimacy had subsisted between our families, and we were much together. Demetrius had never exhibited any particular marks of affection for me, yet I cannot deny that I had for some time cherished a growing preference for the handsome, high-spirited companion of my youth. It was the superstitious feeling I have before mentioned that induced me to consult the Oracle of the Sweet Waters as to how my young passion for Demetrius would thrive; and I returned from my enquiry disconsolate and overpowered, as all the answers of the oracle turned out unfavourable to my hopes. Under the dominion of a long cherished superstition, handed down from generation to generation, and sanctioned by the examples of all around, I would as soon have thought of counteracting the declared decrees of providence as of cherishing a hope in opposition to the oracle. You may suppose my agitation on being informed by my father that he was going to the governor to request permission for our marriage. With trembling anxiety I waited the result. Our governor was a Bashaw of three tails who, although a native of Stampalier and originally a Latin Christian, had long ago changed the cross for the crescent Ali Ozman was the Turkish name he assumed. It is usual, in asking a favour of our governors, to accompany it with a present. The one my father carried with him in support of his petition did not exactly please Ozman (for, of course, my father was afraid of exciting suspicions of his wealth by being too liberal), and Ozman received it with contemptuous indifference. Though he had turned Turk, he had enough of the Latin Christian in him to hate one of the Greek church mortally. My father prostrated himself three times as he presented his offering. 'Is thy daughter handsome, Christian dog?' asked Ozman. At this, a French renegade, who had insinuated himself into the confidence of Ozman, whispered to him that I was the fairest virgin in the isle. Ozman considered a few moments, and said with a smile, 'I accept thy present, and permit thy daughter to wed the young Greek on condition that thou grant a feast before the marriage, and bid me be a guest.' My father returned home in a melancholy mood, and gave direction for the preparation of the feast and the reception of the cruel Ozman. From a sudden recollection of the disastrous omen of the oracle, darker and more dreary became my thoughts than they had ever been since the hour I became convinced Demetrius loved me. He also all that day seemed labouring under a depression, and departed early in the evening oppressed by vague forebodings he could not define. The feast was, however, prepared, the company bidden and, after waiting a considerable time for the arrival of Ozman, who did not appear, the ceremony proceeded with Demetrius and myself each choosing a godfather to attend us. At the altar we were met by the aged papa, or Greek priest, who, after blessing two crowns of foliage intertwined with ribbons and laces, placed them on our heads. He then in like manner blessed two rings, one of silver, the other of gold, placing the former on my finger, the latter on that of Demetrius. After these rings had been exchanged and we had taken our vows, the old priest was preparing to distribute the bread and wine which was to conclude the ceremony when a light strain of Turkish music at a distance caught our attention. In a little while Ozman was seen advancing at the head of twenty or thirty of his guards. Demetrius earnestly besought the priest to finish the ceremony before the barbarians should arrive to interrupt it, but the old man trembled so that the wine was spilled and the consecrated bread fell from his hands. In a few moments Ozman and his train entered the church with their scimitars drawn and scattered the bridal train, leaving me, my father, Demetrius and the priest alone at the altar.

'Stop, dog!' cried Ozman. 'I forbid the marriage in the name of the prophet.'

'It is too late,' replied the old priest, meekly.

'Be silent, Christian dog! Or I will stop thy howlings,' Ozman cried. 'But what is this I smell—wine? You have been carousing, you swine! You have been swilling of that accursed beverage abhorred by Allah, and denounced by his Prophet. It is enough; seize the virgin and trample into dust all that oppose us.' During the whole of the fateful proceedings my poor father supported himself against the side of the smouldering altar in speechless horror. I could not speak, but my eyes were fixed on Demetrius, whose inflexible silence I but too well understood. The youth was too indignant to speak, but the clenched hands, quivering lips and blazing eye spoke a prologue to opposition and vengeance.

'Seize the virgin!' repeated Ozman, 'she will be only too honoured and happy to escape the pollution of this blaspheming wine bibber.' Ozman advanced as he uttered these insulting words. At that instant Demetrius sprang like lightning upon the foremost of the ravishers, and wrenched the scimitar from his hand before he was aware of his purpose. He rushed on Ozman: the first blow made his scimitar fly ringing into the air, the second was arrested by one of the guards, which saved the life of the tyrant, who exclaimed, almost choking with passion, 'He has struck a Mussulman; he has outraged the law of the Prophet; he has polluted the person of the representative of the Commander of the Faithful. Hew him to the earth! Cut him into atoms! Scatter his flesh to the beasts of the field! Let the dogs feed on the Christian reptile!' The crisis was come; my poor father took courage from despair, and seizing upon Ozman's scimitar, which still lay upon the ground, placed himself besides Demetrius, determined to share his fate and the with him. Guess my indescribable anguish. I was seized by several of the guards, whilst others attacked my father and lover. A desperate conflict ensued. My father fought bravely, but soon fell dead by the side of Demetrius, who had rushed towards the tyrant thinking he had him within his power, but a scimitar from behind had cleaved open his head. He sank on the ground never more to rise. At this dreadful sight my senses forsook me, and I do not know how long I continued insensible, for when I was brought back to life I was in a state of raving delirium, in which I have been informed I continued for many weeks. When I finally recovered, I found myself the property of a slave merchant on board a Turkish vessel which was sailing for Tunis. On arriving there I was sold to the Dey. It was at Tunis I learned how I escaped the brutish lust of the villain Ozman. After the slaughter of my father and lover he had me conveyed to his harem, no doubt for the purpose of sacrificing my chastity to his abominable desires; but from the state I was in it became necessary for a doctor to be sent for, and he, after administering such medicines as brought me to myself, instantly declared me to be in a state of complete insanity. By the laws of Mahomet no one, under penalty of death, can abuse or take any liberty with the person of one of unsound mind. Thus for the moment I escaped ravishment. Shortly afterwards, in consequence of some act of peculation the wretch committed, the Sultan caused him to be strangled and his effects to be sold; being found among his slaves I became the property of the slave merchant, who quickly conveyed me from my country, home and friends, well knowing where my person would find a good market.

It appears such as I am I did not exactly strike the taste of the Dey, for he shortly afterwards sent me as a gift to our present master, who it seems it was decreed should enjoy the virgin treasures which the wicked Ozman dared not deprive me of and the Dey of Tunis neglected or did not think worth his time to take from me. After my first interview with the Dey I clearly saw that my chastity was in considerably more danger than it had been while I was in the power of Ozman, and that I was now without the protection I then enjoyed. After my recovery from the dreadful malady with which I was seized at the cruel butchery of my lover and father, a fixed melancholy settled on me in the place of the disorder. This the Dey on seeing me perceived, and he became anxious to know the cause why one so young and beautiful (as he was pleased to describe me) should be afflicted with such a determined lowness of spirits. In compliance with his urgent wishes, I related the history of my misfortunes. During my narrative he sat by my side and took one of my hands in his. I could clearly feel and see by his agitation how much my story affected him; the tear of sensibility stood trembling in his eye at the relation of my sufferings.

When I had finished he drew me trembling to his bosom, and tenderly kissing my forehead, said he blushed that such a villain as Ozman should disgrace the name of Mussulman. 'Have you no relations that I can return you to?' he demanded. I told him I knew of no relation but my father, and he and Demetrius were dead. 'No wonder,' he continued, your beauties are clouded; the misfortunes felt by one so young have been enough to sink you to the very earth. But cheer up, sweet maid, here you shall be free from all importunity. It is true you are my slave, and by our laws I can, if I think fit, violate your beauties; but no. As yet you have experienced nothing but oppression at our hands. I will try by kindness to deserve the enjoyment of your charms.'

Again he pressed me fondly to his bosom, but instead of kissing me as before, my lips received his pressures until their fierceness threw me into a confusion indescribable; but on seeing me in tears he immediately desisted, assuring me that my modesty had nothing to fear from him. But young and inexperienced as I was, nature assured me I had more to fear from the soft pity and seeming sensibility of the amorous Ali than the villainous proceedings of the ferocious Ozman. Ozman might have debauched me by force it is true, but with Ali I had more than force to guard against—I mean nature, which the persuasive Ali, even on my first interview, had contrived to alarm by his kisses, which (I know not why) I scarcely dared to refuse him, particularly as he always desisted when the fervency of his proceedings gave my modesty reason to complain. But I soon became conscious that at each new interview the liberties he took became more daring, so much so that I had determined to request he would send me home to my native isle as he had offered to do.

The very evening I had come to this resolution he sent word by one of his eunuchs that he would take his coffee with me. He came accordingly. After coffee was served (as was his usual custom) he reclined on the sofa, directing me to place myself by his side. I obeyed, as he never had refused to permit my rising when the fear of his proceedings had alarmed me. This evening I though he seemed particularly tender, but somewhat thoughtful. As usual, my lips became his prey. Without my knowledge he contrived to unbutton my bodice at the bosom, and ere I could oppose it his burning hand had invaded and was moulding one of my breasts. This new proceeding threw me into considerable agitation. I requested him to desist; to take his hand away. He immediately complied, merely demanding whether his caresses gave me uneasiness. Indeed so very kind did he appear that evening, I at last summoned up courage to make my request of being sent home. His kindness I confessed I should never forget I supported my petition with all the artless sophistry I was capable of. Ah, I little knew the value of the favour I was soliciting.

At first he seemed much astonished, and I thought affected, but with pleasure I saw the frown fade from his brow. He called me unkind, ungenerous, to wish to desert him at the very moment he had nearly persuaded himself that his attention and forbearance had created a sentiment in my bosom favourable to his hopes. 'Say, sweet maid,' he cried, fondly kissing me, 'you cannot, will not abandon me.' I hardly know how I resisted his pressure and importunities, but I did, and at last received the joyful assurance from him that I should return to my country-home I had none. But his promise was all deception, for even at the very moment he made it, his plans for my ruin were taking effect. Determined on my enjoyment, he had caused to be infused in the coffee which had been handed to me, a strong sleeping draught. Thus at the very moment I was soliciting for the safety of my virtue, my virgin hour was rapidly expiring, and my eyes were growing heavy with the effect of the opium. In fact, sleep overtook me in his arms, and I did not recover from the stupefying quality of the narcotic drug before my virginity and all hopes of escape were destroyed. I was no sooner asleep than the Dey had me undressed and conveyed to bed, whereupon he quickly followed. I became his unresisting prey. The acuteness of the painful sensations which I am told always accompany the transformation of the maid into the finished woman are unknown to me, for so powerful was the medicine that I continued buried all the night in the most profound insensibility—in fact, during all the time the Dey was in uncontrolled possession of my person; indeed so thoroughly had he prepared me to meet his pleasures when I should recover my senses, that during his first enjoyment of me, when perfectly awake, I felt not the least sensation that could be possibly called painful. You may guess my astonishment and sorrow, on awakening from my deathlike stupor, to find myself naked in the arms of the Dey, who was fast asleep, his head reclining on my bosom. From a certain stiffness I felt in a particular part, the truth crashed upon my mind instantly. I could not refrain from crying aloud, which awoke the Dey. He was not slow in pleading an excuse for what he had done, stating that, burning for my enjoyment, and plainly seeing my invincible modesty would oppose the most strenuous resistance to the completion of his desires, he determined, by rendering me insensible to my seduction, to spare my feelings and blushes.

'How could you suppose, lovely creature,' he cried, passionately, 'that it was possible I could part with charms like yours? Where would you fly to? No one to protect you—no home! Your beauties are too great to suffer you long to escape the snares which some brutal renegade like Ozman would set to trap you. Then, sweet slave, pardon my offence; in me you will always find a kind and faithful protector. Come, dry those lovely eyes,' he continued; 'no longer rend my heart with those agonising looks.' In this manner, joined with the softest caresses, did Ali strive to soothe me after giving my first burst of passion its free vent. What he said was very true. I had no home or friend. Where was I to fly to? My state of wretchedness was too apparent. It required very little reflection to convince me the grand ordeal was past, my virginity being his. In short, he soothed me with the soft asseverations of the tenderest love, giving his persuasions with the most lively caresses, until at last by degrees he stemmed the tide of sorrow that flowed over my feelings. Seeing my grief was somewhat pacified, he considered this a fit opportunity to begin to prepare me to submit to his desires. I was entirely unconscious of his intentions. He suddenly turned me on my back, forcibly extended my thighs with one of his knees and in an instant was secure between them; without further ceremony he fixed himself in me, and vigorously making play, his quick thrusts soon sent him in fierce erection to his utmost length into me; indeed, I felt him up to the very quick; I was literally gorged by him. You may suppose my astonishment at finding the insertion of his instrument unaccompanied by the least particle of pain. [I interrupted her by enquiring if she felt not the least suffering.] None whatever, and I can only attribute it to the number of times he must have enjoyed me while I was under the influence of the opiate, for

I assure you the pains accompanying the loss of virginity are entirely unknown to me. Nay, on the contrary, I felt not the least inconvenience. So you may guess my emotions at the awful moment when he had driven himself into me, joining as it were our bodies into one by the close junction of the parts. My hands were clenched—my whole body immovable—my teeth, fixed. I was lost to everything but the wonderful instrument that was sheathed within me. I call it wonderful, and I think not improperly; for wonderful must that thing be that in the midst of the most poignant grief can so rapidly dissolve our senses with the softest sensations, spite of inclination, so quickly cause us to forget our early impressions, our first affections, and in the most forlorn and wretched moments of our existence make us taste such voluptuous delight and lustful pleasure! This was my case. At the very moment I thought myself the most wretched of all human beings did the Dey, by his luxurious movements, cause me to experience the most sensual of all enjoyments, which every instant became more and more poignant and dissolving, until I was completely ravished with unutterable delight. I unconsciously grasped him in my arms, unable to conceal the joys I was convulsed with; and soon in my agony of bliss, amounting to little less than delirium, did I feel spouting from him the milk of life, which rushed in delicious streams into my womb, and quickly drew down from me with shuddering ecstasy my maiden tribute of the melting essence. After the first ecstasy, as he lay in my arms, whilst I was still languishing from the joy I had experienced, did he extract from me an unqualified kiss of forgiveness for his deceit and treachery, and on my lips did he seal an oath to Allah never to desert me. I now became passive if not resigned to my fate. Drawing his shaft out of me, and removing himself from between my thighs, he informed me that in the evening when his strength was sufficiently recruited, it was his intention to give me my finishing instructions in love's mysteries; for as yet, though it was evident to him I had enjoyed the pleasure, yet I had much to learn and to do ere (as he said) I could enjoy the ecstasy properly. He then left me. I shall not tire you with an account of how I passed the day; it is sufficient to say that towards evening the female slaves, after having conducted me to the bath, and properly ornamented my hair, and every way prepared me, helped me into bed to await the Dey's coming. He came covered only by a robe, which thrown off left him entirely naked, and he came to bed to me. If I had any repugnance left, this might certainly have removed it entirely. Directly he was laid by my side he first threw off the bedclothes, then untying the ribbons which closed my dress in front, he threw it open, leaving my person naked to his view. He then examined every part of me, covering me as he did so with numberless kisses. Having satisfied his curiosity as to my person, he drew me to his bosom, and desired me to place my lips to his. He then taught me several ways of kissing. The first was merely drawing my lips softly across his, which he called dove-kissing. The second was keeping my lips glued to his, returning his suction until he withdrew his lips: this he called the kiss of enjoyment; and the third was the same with the difference of thrusting his tongue into my mouth—this was described by him as the kiss of desire.

When he thought he had sufficiently taught me the manner of kissing which pleased him, he desired me particularly to remember that whenever he got between my thighs I must immediately extend them to their utmost width, and when I found he had completely entered me, then, and not till then, I was to embrace his body with my arms, and pass my lips softly over his when I felt him beginning to thrust; as he withdrew out of me, I was also to withdraw from him, but not so much as to throw him out; and as he thrust home again, I was also to meet him with all my force, my arms all the time encircling him firmly—all my kisses to be entirely governed by his manner of kissing, and immediately I felt him beginning to discharge himself within me, I was instantly to throw my legs over his back and keep myself immovably fixed in the closest junction with him, until the very last drop was ejected from him; but, above all, he particularly pressed upon me to obey him in everything he directed implicitly, assuring me I should find my reward in obedience. With blushes I promised to obey his desires in every particular. He then got between my thighs, which I extended to his wishes; this I saw gratified him; then, on his knees between them, he desired me to take hold of his instrument, and pass my hand up and down it two or three times. I did as he directed, but could not look him in the face. Ah, I could scarcely grasp the stately pillar! As my hand slipped up and down it, I felt it throb and leap freely. I was struck with astonishment at how I could have entertained so superb and magnificent a shaft! I was not given long to consider about it. He laid himself down on me; with his left hand he unclosed the luscious lips of the mouth of nature, while with the right he bent his mighty instrument—so stiff was its erection that he appeared with difficulty to force it down to the opening—and presently I felt its broad shelving head entering between the lips which the fingers kept extended. When he got in, as if he meant to spin out his pleasure and give it more play, he passed his instrument up so slowly that it appeared an age to me until I had fairly received it into the soft laboratory of love. At last our mossy mounts fairly rubbed against each other. But ah! How silly were the directions he had given me as to not embracing him until this moment! It was out of my power to resist the impulse I felt. If my life had depended upon it I could not have forborne from grasping him to my breast. As to his other directions, I believe I gave him perfect satisfaction. At first I was passive by force, but as he made play, the in-and-out friction soon awakened, touched and roused me to the quick, so that, unable to contain myself, I could not but comply with his motions as quickly as the delicacy of my make and my inexperience would admit of, until the pleasure rose to such a height that it made me wild with ravishing sensations, in fact I threw my legs about at random, entirely lost in the sweet agitation. As to the Dey, his ecstasy declared itself by the increasing quickness and fierceness of his thrusts, his rough grasping of my body, his burning kisses and eyes darting humid fires. As the last moment, the critical moment came, I had barely sufficient recollection to follow my instructions. I instantly entwined my legs over his loins, every part of us was strictly joined, and, oh God! he distilled into me a flood of rapture which was met by me, I scarcely know how, for the transport was so great that I actually fainted in his arms.

When I recovered, the endearing language and tender caresses of the Dey fully spoke his entire satisfaction, and from that moment I became his favourite slave; so I continued until you were brought into the harem. But pray, Madame [she said, tenderly throwing herself into my arms and kissing me], do not think me jealous of your superior attractions, for although in our unfortunate situations the pleasures of the Dey's embraces are an extreme source of consolation as well as gratification, yet I assure you [her beautiful eyes filled with tears as she spoke] no one but Demetrius could ever make me jealous. Demetrius was my true, my only love.

# Letter 8

Emily Barlow to Sylvia Carey (continued)


I had forgot to mention before the unhappy fate of my companion Eliza, whom I never saw after my first introduction to the Dey; she was presented by the Dey to the Dey of Tunis, whose shocking barbarity to his female slaves was the common gossip of our harem. One day the Dey came into my room, and throwing down a letter, told me it contained all the particulars of the ravishment of my friend, adding, 'She has had a little worse treatment than my slaves generally meet with.'


I seized the letter, and you may judge my feelings on reading the following:

Letter
9

## The Dey of Tunis to the Dey of Algiers

A pretty trick you have played me. By Mahomet's beard, it is abominable! To look at her, who would have credited it? Such a meek-eyed, timid-looking thing! By Allah, Ali, merely for thrusting my hands into her breasts did she fly at me like a tiger, and my face was instantly furrowed by her cursed nails like unto a field new ploughed. But I wrong you to suppose you could have known what a termagant she was; if you had, you certainly would have communicated the character of your present. I may properly say she was a termagant for she is now tamed. When somewhat recovered from the surprise her sudden attack created, I summoned some of the eunuchs, into whose care I delivered her, determined to defer my revenge until the wounds of my face were healed—and you shall hear how then this vixen was subdued.

In a few days my face was well; my directions that she should be treated with every possible respect in the meantime had quite put her off her guard. One morning the eunuchs conveyed her to my experiment room, where, before she could tell what they were about, her hands were securely fastened together and drawn above her head, through a pulley fixed in the ceiling. I directed her to be pulled up so as not to lift her off the ground, but that she should not be able to throw herself down. When this was effected I entered the room and dismissed the eunuchs. There she stood trembling with rage, but unable to help herself. I now drew a couch towards her, and having seated myself close to her, placed one arm around her waist, and with the other was about to lift up her clothes.

It is impossible to describe the exertions she made to prevent my proceedings, she twisted herself about and writhed and kicked until I was obliged to abandon my attempt for a moment and call in the eunuchs, who quickly (in spite of her kicking) secured each of her feet to a ring placed in the floor, about two feet and a half from each other. This, of course, considerably extended her legs and thighs. She was then secure every way. After dismissing the eunuchs, I again drew the couch close to her, and without further ceremony lifted up her clothes. Oh, Ali, what delicious transport shot through my veins at the voluptuous charms exhibited to my ardent gaze! How lovely was her round mount of love, just above the temple of Venus, superbly covered with beautiful black hair, how soft and smooth as ivory her belly and her swelling, delicately formed thighs! The cygnet down instantly disclosed that she was a maid, for where the bodies have been properly joined in the fierce encounter, the hair (particularly of the female) loses that sleek downy appearance, and by the constant friction the smooth hair becomes rubbed into delightful little curls. But, to put the fact beyond dispute, I thrust my forefinger into the little hole below. Her loud cries, and the difficulty of entering which was found, set the fact beyond dispute. Immediately dropping on my knees, grasping in each hand one of her buttocks, I placed on her virgin toy a most delicious kiss. I then got up and began to undress her. She appeared nearly choked with passion; her tears flowed down her beautiful face in torrents. But her rage was of no use. Proceeding leisurely, first taking off one thing, then another, and with the help of scissors, I quickly rid her of every covering.

Holy Mahomet! What a glorious sight she exhibited: beautiful breasts-finely placed, sufficiently firm to support themselves—shoulders, belly, thighs, legs, everything was deliriously voluptuous! But what most struck my fancy was the beautiful whiteness, roundness and voluptuous swell of firm flesh of her lovely buttocks and thighs. 'Soon,' I said to myself, handling her delicious bum, 'soon shall this lovely whiteness be mixed with a crimson blush!' I placed burning kisses upon every part of her; wherever my lips travelled instantly the part was covered with scarlet blushes. Having directed two rods to be placed on the couch, also a leather whip with broad lashes, I took one of the rods and (shoving the couch out of the way) began gently to lay it on the beautiful posterior of my sobbing captive. At first I did it gently enough—it could have no other effect than just to tickle her; but shortly I began every now and then to lay on a smart lash, which made her wince and cry out. This tickling and cutting I kept up for some time—until the alabaster cheeks of her bum had become suffused with a slight blush—then suddenly I began to give the rod with all my might; then indeed was every lash followed by a cry, or an exclamation for pity, such as 'Oh! spare me, for God's sake! have pity on me! you cut me in pieces!'

'Ah, I cannot bear it! I shall die!' Her winces and the delicious wiggling of her backside increased in proportion to the increase of the force of my lashes and these continued, heedless of her cries, entreaties and complaints, until both the rods and myself were exhausted. To recover breath I drew the couch close to her and seated myself; the entire surface of her beautiful buttocks was covered with welts; every here and there, where the stem of the leaves had caught her, appeared a little spot of crimson blood, which went trickling down the lily thighs. Again and again did I slide my hand over her numerous beauties. Again and again did my forefinger intrude itself into her delicate little hole of pleasure. She could not avoid anything I thought fit to do. Her thighs were stretched wide enough for me to have enjoyed her if I had thought fit, but that was not my immediate intention. I had settled she was to receive the quantity of punishment allotted her before she was deflowered.

Having recovered my breath, I stripped myself, and, seizing the leather whip, began to flog her with such effect that the blood followed every lash. Vain were her cries and supplications—still lash followed lash in rapid succession. I was now in so princely a state of erection that I could have made a hole where there had been none before, let alone drive myself into a place which nature had been so bountiful as to form of stretching material. Quickly summoning the eunuchs, I directed them to lay her on her back on the couch, properly securing an arm on each side to one of the legs of the couch. It was accomplished as quickly as ordered. They retired, leaving me with my exhausted victim to complete the sacrifice. I was not long in rooting up her modesty, deprived as she was of the use of her arms and exhausted by her sufferings. A pillow having been placed under her sufficiently to raise her bottom so as to leave a fair mark for my engine, I threw her legs over my shoulders, and softly (as a tender mother playing with her infant) opened the lips of paradise and love to reveal its coral hue and mossy little grotto—and each fold closed upon the intruding finger, repelling the unwelcome guest. Inconceivable is the delight one feels in these transporting situations! There is nothing on earth so much enhances the joy with me as to know the object that affords me the pleasure detests me, but cannot help from satisfying my desires—her tears and looks of anguish are sources of unutterable joy to me! Being satisfied in every way, by sight, by touch, by every sense, that I was the first possessor, I placed the head of my instrument between the distended lips, grasping her thighs with her legs over my shoulders, then making a formidable thrust, lodged the head entirely in her; she turned her beautiful eyes up to heaven as if looking there for assistance—

her exhaustion precluded any opposition; another fierce thrust deepened the insertion; tears in torrents followed my efforts, but she disdained to speak; still I thrust, but no complaint; but growing fiercer, one formidable plunge proved too mighty for her forbearance—she not only screamed, but struggled. However, I was safely in her. Another thrust finished the job; it was done, and nobly done, by Mahomet! Europa was never half so well unvirgined, although love might have had the strength of a bull. After having cooled my burning passion by a copious discharge, I withdrew myself. Crimson tears followed my exit; with a handkerchief I wiped away the precious drops, and falling on my knees between her thighs, placed on the torn and wounded lips a delicious kiss—delicious beyond measure. Only consider, Ali, to know beyond dispute that no one but myself had divided these pouting, fresh, warm, clasping and gaping gates of pleasure! Indeed it was rapturous beyond description. I now thought it time to untie the silken cord that confined the arms of this young vixen. On feeling her arms released, her only motion was to cover her eyes with her hands; there she lay on her back immovable—but for her sobs I could not have told whether she existed. I left her, but ordered the eunuchs to convey her to her apartments, directing the greatest care to be taken of her until my return from an excursion I was about to make to Bona.

I was gone twelve days. During my journey, I had refrained from women, consequently on my return I felt myself in an extremely amorous mood. Not intending to give her modesty (if she had any left) an excuse for resistance, I directed her to be again secured, but this time I had her fastened face downwards to a curious couch made on purpose, at the end of which, by means of a handle, the positions may be elevated or lowered to any height convenient. On lifting up her clothes, to my great joy I found there was not the least remains of the flagellation so liberally administered to her. Her swelling ivory thighs and voluptuous firm buttocks had perfectly recovered their beautiful freshness. I think it is utterly impossible for anyone to possess charms exceeding in beauty the rising plumpness of her lovely limbs! How delightful the touch and squeeze of her bum! After tucking her clothes securely up as high as the small of her back, so that her twisting could not unloosen them, I undressed myself, and arming myself with a magnificent rod, commenced giving her a second lesson in birch discipline. Not intending this bout to make her suffer much, having (as I said) completely broken her spirit when I deflowered her, all that I now intended was to enjoy the luxurious wriggling, plunging and kicking which usually attends a smart flagellation. From the tears that already filled her beautiful eyes, I plainly perceived she expected the same treatment she had before experienced; but she was deceived—for this time I did not lay into her with more strength than was necessary to cover her posterior with a slight carnation blush. But still the delicious struggles and writhes, as the expected cat fell upon her round buttocks, threw me into so luxurious a frenzy that it caused me soon to abandon the rod. By means of the wheel and handle I raised her buttocks until her delicate little hole of pleasure was properly placed to receive me. I directed myself to the entrance. Having thoroughly stretched her on my first attack, three or four thrusts were enough to engulf my fullest length into her; in fact she sustained the insertion without making any great complaint, only a little cry or so. Nothing adds to the enjoyment so much as the active reciprocation of the female when she returns the transport; when that return is not willingly given, its place must be supplied in the best way available. It could hardly be expected that any return would be made by my captive, consequently I was obliged to make the best substitute I could; so, seizing her round the loins as I drove myself into her, grasping her close and drawing her towards me, I made her meet the coming thrusts, thus famously supplying the want of her own free will in the exertions of my pleasures. Master of the place, I gave way with all my energy to the voluptuous joys with which my senses were surrounded. At every fierce insertion my stones slapped against the soft lips of her delicate slit. Everything conspired to excite, to gratify my senses. Driving close into her, I for a moment stopped my furious thrusts to play with the soft silly hair which covered her mount of love; then slipping my hand over her ivory belly up to her breasts, I made her rosy nipples my next prey. Then, Ali, I again commenced my ravishing in-and-out strokes. Oh, how beautiful was the sight in the mirror by my side, as I drew myself out of her, of the rosy lips of her sheath protruding out clasping my instrument as if fearing to lose it! then again, as the column returned up to the quick, to see the crimson edging that surrounded me gradually retreating inwards, until it was entirely lost in the black circles of her mossy hair! In short, Ali, overcome with voluptuous sensations, the crisis seized me. I distilled, as it were, my very soul into her! Satisfied, I now withdrew myself, then releasing her hands, I stripped her of her clothes (all but her shift) and carried her to a more commodious couch, on which I threw her, and placed myself by her side. She had now nothing to lose. Fear, no doubt, prevented her making resistance to my proceedings. The view and touch of so many beauties again fired my blood. I seized her, threw myself upon her, divided her thighs, quickly buried myself in her, and again and again drowned myself in a sea of sensual delight, in which it must be confessed the sweet girl did not to appearances participate. But in my next I hope to give a better account of her.

MUZRA

This letter you may be assured made me feel quite unhappy. While on this subject I will give you the contents of the subsequent letter, written about a week afterwards.

Letter
10

Muzra to Ali

Ah, Ali, the English slave has indeed been a fatal present to your friend. You will scarcely credit the dreadful recompense she has taken for her lost virginity.

Yes, Ali, nothing but my life would satisfy her. Doubtless her wishes will be gratified, for I feel life ebbing fast from me. As I informed you in my last, I supposed that her spirit was quite subdued; but I little knew the mind I had to contend with, or how terrible a retribution she would exact for my trespass on her charms! But I must quickly finish. Several times I had enjoyed her in the daytime, but had not slept with her. One night, truly fatal for me, I ordered the eunuchs to bring her to my sleeping apartment. Oh, Ali, nothing could exceed the docility, mixed with the timid bashfulness of her behaviour. In the midst of my joys she clasped me in her arms, returning my kisses as ardently as they were given, and appearing to receive as much ecstatic pleasure as she herself gave. But it was all deceit, to lull me to my destruction. Wearied by bliss, I sank by her side into a delightful slumber, from which I was awoken by the piercing of a knife through my bosom. It was daylight; she was leaning over me with a savage joy, brandishing the fatal instrument that had already pierced me. Again it fell on my defenseless bosom. 'That's for my lost virtue!' she cried. Again she struck me, 'That's for my cruel scourging!' And again flourishing it before my eyes, she cried, 'Receive that for the many times you have forced my poor body to submit to your loathsome pollutions.' Again it fell unerring on my breast. I shrieked aloud for help.

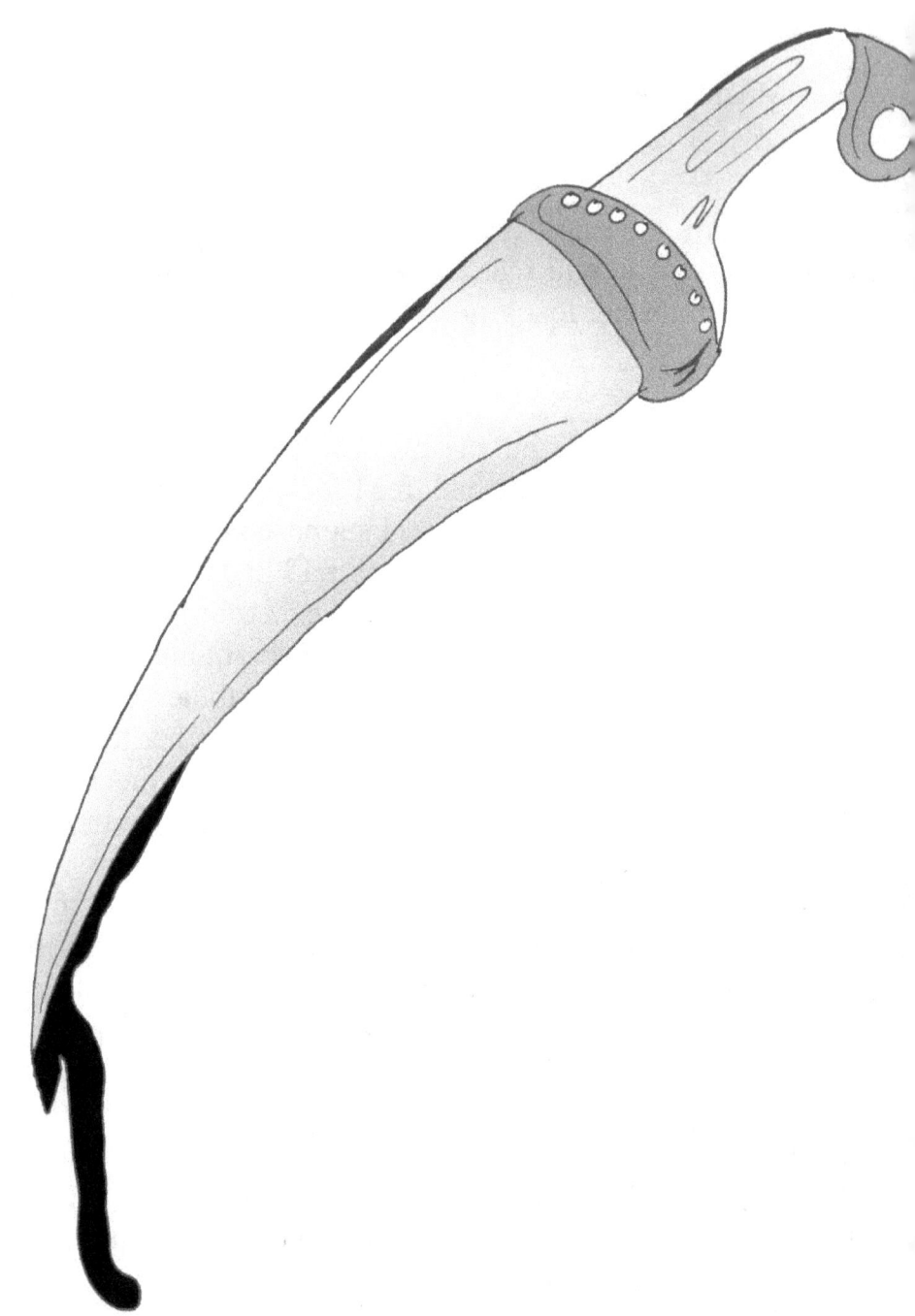

Two of the eunuchs rushed in. She had sprung out of bed. The first (who attempted to seize her) paid with his life the forfeit of temerity, but the other overpowered her. Weak from the loss of blood, I had still strength enough to order she should not be hurt. My orders were obeyed. To prevent any ill usage to her in case I should not recover, I have sent her back to you. I can dictate no more at present. If I should depart to Paradise, as you respect your friend, let no one injure her. Farewell. May happiness attend you.

MUZRA


I can hardly describe my feelings on reading this last letter. I was pleased to think Eliza has returned, for I am in hopes now of having some of her company. I have asked the Dey to permit her to visit me, and he has promised me that I shall be gratified. The Dey of Tunis is recovering from his wounds, but will not, I presume, want Eliza back again, for fear of her taking further vengeance on him. Adieu, dearest Sylvia.

EMILY BARLOW

# Letter
## 11

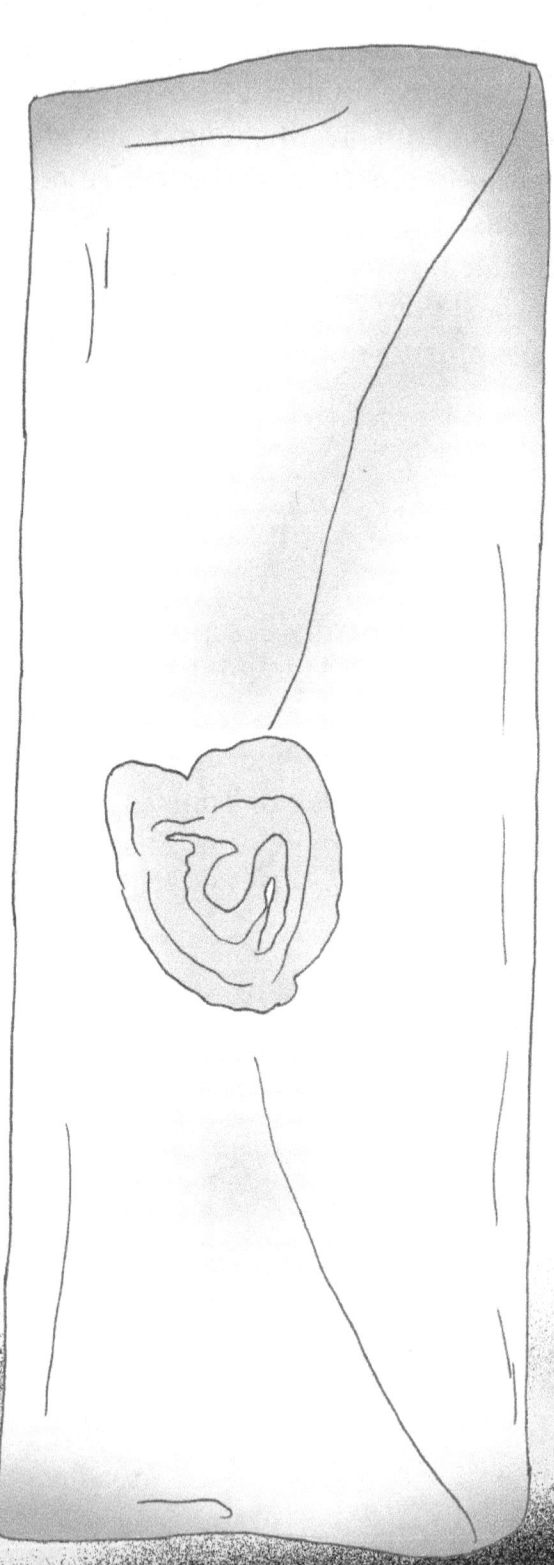

Sylvia Carey to Emily Barlow

Toulon, France

Emily—

It is impossible at once to shake off our earliest acquaintance; if it had been you ought not to have expected that I should have taken any notice of your disgusting letters. What offence have I ever given that you should insult me by writing in the language you have? Why annoy me with an account of the libidinous scenes acted between you and the beast whose infamous and lustful acts you so particularly describe? Did I not know the character of your writing well, I should be in hopes I was deceived by some wretch. But no, every part of your writing carries conviction. I have to thank God the letters fell into my hands, else your infamy would have dragged another crime on your guilty head by the death of my unfortunate brother who most certainly would have fallen under the dreadful discovery if he had by accident gone (which he most usually does) to the post office for our letters. Although the letters were directed to me, he would assuredly have opened them had he seen your writing. But thank God this pang has at present been spared him. After you sailed from Portsmouth, Henry's health became daily worse, and the physicians declared that nothing but a warmer climate would save his life. I was therefore determined to pass the summer in the South of France and the neighbourhood of this place was fixed upon for our residence. Your mother determined to accompany us. We made the journey by stages, and on arriving here hired a most delightful cottage, a short walk outside the fortifications of the town, opposite the sea. Here Henry's health has daily improved, and both our parents are in hopes of his entire recovery. The time when he expects to hear from you in India is not yet expired, so at present he is easy on this point. God knows what the result will be when he hears of your debased situation, and the infamous satisfaction it gives you! Your mother is the only person I have dared to communicate the sad tidings to, and we have given particular direction to the postmaster at Toulon not to permit Henry to have any letters directed to either of us. We therefore feel sure that none of your letters can fall into his hands. I cannot describe your mother's grief, which she is obliged to hide from my brother; it is evidently making rapid inroads on her constitution. I am enabled to write to you direct as a vessel is now leaving for the port of Algiers with some missionaries on board for the redemption of slaves; but the nature of your letters has so distracted your mother that she does not know how to proceed, or whether it is your wish to be released from the infamous subjection in which your beastly ravisher seems to hold both your person and senses. If there is a spark of feeling, on your mother's account (or modesty on your own) left, make no delay in letting me know if you wish to escape from the wretch who thus holds you in his thraldom. I subscribe myself still your friend (if you deserve it),


SYLVIA CAREY


This letter was written before the receipt of Emily's last letter.

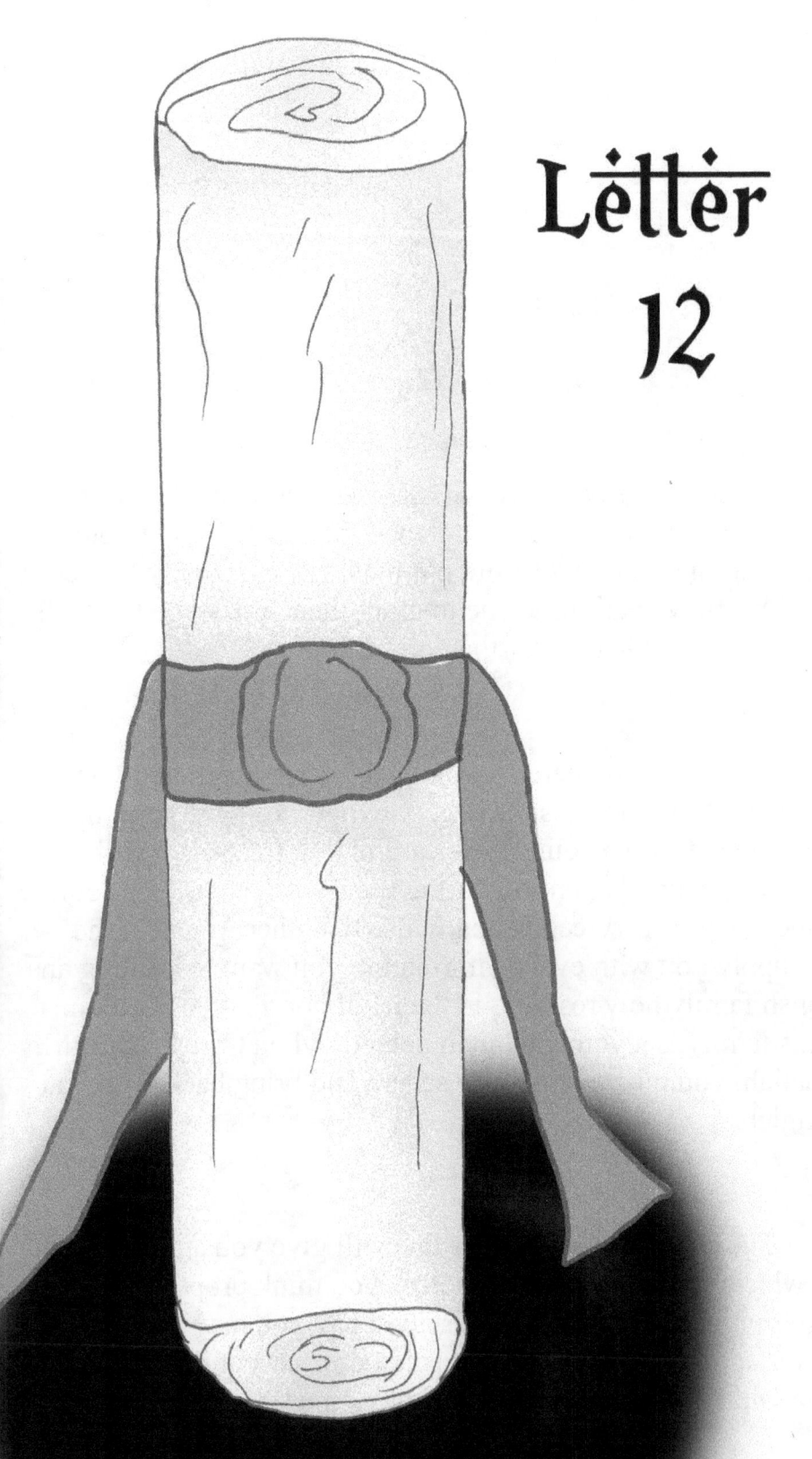

Letter
12

## The Dey to Abdallah

Abdallah—

A short time back several missionaries arrived here from the South of France since their arrival they have been employed in redeeming several worn-out old male slaves, mostly Frenchmen. They have petitioned me to grant them a passage home in the first ship that leaves for the port of Toulon.

For the reason herein explained, I have appointed you to carry them to France. As these holy hypocrites have great influence in their own country, be careful you treat them with the proper respect and attention during their voyage, as their countenance may be serviceable, particularly Father Angelo, who will supply you with every information you want respecting an English family now residing in the neighbourhood of Toulon. In this family is a young woman named Sylvia Carey. This girl, Abdallah, you must contrive to secure and bring back with you to Algiers.

The eunuch who delivers this will give you a private signet, which you may show as soon as you think proper to Father Angelo; it will command his services, and you may rely implicitly upon everything the Christian dog says or does. Mind, Abdallah, I have set my mind on having possession of the girl;

do not return without her. Name your own reward, but be careful she is mine.


ALI

# Letter 13

Pedro to Angelo

Angelo—

You remember my informing you of the young and
lovely daughter of the Marquis of Mezzia having been forced
to take the veil in our neighbouring Ursuline Convent. It now
appears this beautiful creature has become a sacrifice to the
pride of the family; its revenue being comparatively beggarly,
no fortune could be given with her in marriage, so there was no
choice. Either the brother must have been reduced to the necessity of seeking a support by some profession (or other means
equally disgusting to the pride of the old Marquis), or this
young innocent must be sacrificed. I need not explain to you,
who was so long the confessor of the late Marquis, the poverty
and pride of both him and young Mezzia. Paternal feeling or
any other social tie which should have protected and supported the beauteous flower, all sank before the imaginary stain
that might be inflicted on the honour of the house by curtailing
the means of one of its descendants. This quickly decided the
proud, unfeeling father and cruel brother, so at the age of seventeen, all her young beauties just ripening into perfection, was
the almost broken-hearted Julia Mezzia forced to utter oaths her
heart abhorred, devoting her voluptuous charms to the service
of religioncharms, Angelina, only fit for the service of vigorous
man.

As I before gave you the full particulars of the distressing
ceremony, I need not revert to it. But although beauty may be

strictly confined by walls and bars, nature will still assume its mighty empire. This lovely virgin has been caught in an attempt to escape from the horrors of a cell for life. She was taken in the act of descending the wall, being betrayed by a sister of the convent, to whom in youthful confidence she had imparted her design. The penalty is death, unless mercy can be purchased for her; but such means as is necessary I do not think the Mezzia family can command, and if they could I shall take care with his Holiness that it has no effect.

You see, Angelo, this blushing rose must be mine. She will be shortly brought to her trial and condemned by the abbess to be buried alive. A report will then be forwarded to the grand vicar, who will procure his Holiness's fiat. It will be my duty to prevent any petitions in her favour being heard. Fare thee well! You will soon hear of my success.

PEDRO,

ABBOT OF ST FRANCIS

# Letter 14

Pedro to Angelo

She is mine, soul and body mine. I have the delicious
angel safe in my secret apartments in the convent, where uncontrolled I revel and feed upon her thrilling beauties. She came
to my fierce embrace a blushing, timid maid. Oh, Angelo, how
delicious were the moments spent in unravelling the Gordian
knot of her coy chastity! How sweet to the ear was the soft cry
that announced the expiration of her virginity. Angelo (believe
me when I write it), the very moment I saw the parlour grating
close upon the lovely Mezzia on the afternoon she received the
veil, a prophetic spirit whispered in mine ear, 'She is mine.'
She is mine—only mine—wholly mine. Nearly the whole of
last night was I voluptuously encircled by her wary limbs, her
young budding breasts rapturously beating against my manly
bosom, her glowing cheek fondly pressed to mine, and only
removed to resign her balmy lips to my burning kisses. Night
of exquisite rapture! May it never be weakened in the tablet
of memory! As I predicted, Angelo, for her attempt to escape
from the convent, the austere Abbess of St Ursuline immediately called a chapter to try this lovely disgrace to our holy
religion. Her friends were notified of her infamous attempt, and
in due time the trial took place, in the presence of her father,
brother and friends. Sister Sophia, the nun in whom my young
pupil had misplaced her confidence, was the principal evidence
against her. It appears before she was excluded from the world
an attachment had subsisted between her and a young noble-
man, whose name was the only thing Julia had not acquainted
Sister Sophia with. As he luckily escaped in the confusion of
securing Julia, he has nothing to fear. The poor girl had no

defense. The detection was too public. What she urged in mitigation of her fault not only incensed the abbess more and more against her, but absolutely caused her father and brother to deny and abandon her to her fate altogether.

She publicly avowed that she was compelled to take the veil by her father and brother, and called on heaven to witness the truth of her assertion and protect her in her distress. Her father and brother fled the convent venting curses on her, and she was condemned by the chapter to be buried alive. Oh, Angelo, how great was my joy at hearing this sentence. You are the only one of the order to whom I have communicated the fact of the existence of a subterraneous passage from my dormitory to the tomb of death in the convent of St Ursuline. Guess with what impatience I waited the result of the case from Rome. The sentence of the chapter being confirmed, the following day was appointed for depositing the victim in the dreadful sepulchre. In the meantime, I descended and conveyed by our subterraneous entrance a comfortable mattress and other conveniences, and I also cleaned out the dungeon of the filth and vermin, so that the tender girl should be able at least to sleep without interruption during the time I intended she should stay there; that you may be sure would be no longer than to make her thankful to surrender her person to my desires when I afforded her an opportunity to escape from death by starvation. I shall not disgust you with an account of the ceremony of forcing this young creature down the marble jaws of the tomb opened in the Ursuline church. Suffice it to say that a rope of sufficient length was fixed firmly round her waist, and, in spite of her struggles and screams, she was carried and held over the dreadful opening and then gradually lowered into the frightful abyss, her cries making the church echo, until the marble slab enclosed her, as it was supposed, from the world forever. I had placed by the side of the mattress sufficient provisions to last her for a day, intending to leave her to reflection for about two or three days; by that time I had no doubt hunger and fear would have so reduced her that to escape from her horrid prison she would quickly submit to any terms I should propose.

On the third day of the incarceration, after vespers, I took my dark lantern and again trod the subterraneous passage. On arriving at the secret entrance of the tomb, I waited a considerable time ere I could ascertain whether she was awake. At last I was assured she slept. With caution I opened the door and silently approached the unconscious sleeper. Removing the shade off the light by degrees, I turned it on her face, fearing to awaken her by letting it flash instantly on her. Poor girl! How evident was the inroad of care and despair on her lovely countenance. She lay her full length on the mattress, her head resting on her right arm, her beautiful tresses playing in confusion over her ivory neck, while the disorder of her veil only half concealed her young, delicious breasts. Her cheeks still retained the traces of recent tears, and her slumbers were disturbed with the horrors of her situation, for unknowingly she uttered, 'Oh, Father, save me!' her whole frame becoming convulsed with the agony even in her dream. I could bear this no longer, but shading my light, coughed loud enough to break the bonds of sleep.

'What noise was that?' exclaimed the poor sufferer. 'I thought I heard someone move. Oh, no, it was the deception of my giddy brain. Alas, there is no hope for a wretch like me!'

I seized this opportunity and slowly uttered the word 'Hope.'

A faint scream, evidently mixed with pleasure, followed my response. After a few second's silence she exclaimed, 'Oh, pray do not play with my wretchedness! If there is anyone near do not drive to despair a miserable girl!'

'Help is nigh,' was my reply. 'But let not joy deceive you with hopes that may not be fulfilled, your release from death depends entirely upon your submission to certain terms.'

'Oh, for heaven's sake name them,' she cried; 'keep me not thus in agonising suspense! Say what I am to do to save myself from the dreadful lingering anguish of famine I now so powerfully feel.'

'Listen,' I replied, 'the only terms upon which you can be released from this den of horrors and certain lingering death is the entire submission of your person to enjoyment; this is the only way you can be saved.' At this moment I unshaded my lamp, and let it reflect full on my face. She covered her eyes with her hands, but she did not answer. 'Come,' I cried, 'time wears apace, you must be quick in your resolve, if I leave this dungeon your fate is fixed forever.' Still there was no answer. I again covered the lamp and solemnly said, 'Well then, farewell,' and moved from her as if I were leaving the tomb.

'Oh, save me,' she cried, believing I was going.

'Well then, you consent to submit to my desires—to every desire or request I choose to make?'

'Oh, yes, everything; save me from death, I will submit to anything.'

'Then you are saved,' I replied, approaching and taking her in my arms. Her soft lips I drew to mine, and sucking her perfumed breath, I sealed our contract. I now told her it was sometimes the case that the abbess would cause the marble covering to be removed from the tomb to point out to any disobedient nuns the punishment that might await them, therefore her clothes must be laid immediately under the opening that they might be seen. Should such event occur, the depth of the tomb would prevent any possibility of ascertaining whether she was in them, else an immediate search might be made in the tomb, and perhaps her retreat eventually discovered, in which case the power of the church would drag her back to her punishment. I again uncovered my lantern and could clearly see her modesty struggling with her fears. Therefore I told her there must be no delay made. 'Come, come,' I cried; 'we must depart this moment, you must yield to the necessity of plucking off your habit.' She trembled, and said she could not think of being naked, with a confusion which made her look on the escape as scarcely a recompense for the shame she must undergo. No doubt she would have debated the proprietary of it, but I peremptorily cut her short by beginning to get rid of her dress by degrees, getting off one thing, then another, until she was wholly stripped of everything. For the trouble I took in her toilet I rewarded myself as I proceeded. I laid her dress at full length on the ground immediately under the opening of the vault, so that it could plainly be perceived from above bearing the appearance of covering a body. I then fixed a handkerchief over the eyes of Julia, and taking her round the waist, led her out of the vault. In a few minutes she was safe in my private apartments, where a table well laid out with every kind of refreshment awaited her. Carrying her to the sofa by the side of the table, I gently laid her on it, and taking off the bandage from her eyes, with a loving kiss assured her of her safety. Although I well knew she must have been suffering considerably from hunger at the time, still I could not refrain from indulging myself with a few moments' toying with her young beauties ere I permitted her to satisfy nature's wants. It is true as I conducted her through the subterraneous passage, every part of her delicate body had been felt by my eager hands, but that you know, Angelo, was in the dark. Now I had her in my arms, every charm was exposed to the broad glare of day. The unrivalled whiteness of her skin was emphasised by the black velvet of the sofa on which she was laid. Quickly my daring hand seized her most secret treasure, regardless of her soft complaints, which my burning kisses reduced to mcre murmurs, while my fingers penetrated into the covered way of love. How transporting is the combat between coy modesty and newborn pleasure. How delicious appears the first blushes of shame on the snowy purity of the virgin's bosom. Ah! Angelo, do you not envy my joys? Guess how I dissolved as my lips wandered over her sweet body! How soft were her cries of 'Ah!' and 'Fie!' I discerned a bright falling tear, but it was the tear of pleasure. Then she tried (but in vain) to remove my hand, whilst her closed eyes clearly told the soft languor was gently creeping on her senses. I scarcely know how to account for my not at that moment exacting my recompense for saving her from the jaws of death. But I did not. I suddenly desisted, and raising her from the position I held her in, drew the table towards the couch, desired she would assist herself to what she thought fit and left the apartment. In my bedroom I had some fine chemises, one of which I brought her and assisted her to put on; it was quite large enough, but of course it was no defense to my curious hands, which I could easily slip to any part of her I pleased. However, I did not interrupt her during her repast, but attended to her wants with the greatest care, forcing her to take two or three glasses of mulled wine, which was already prepared. As the cravings of her appetite were assuaged, mine were every minute growing more furious. Seeing she had finished, although she pretended still to be eating, I gently encircled my arm around her neck; I drew this soft, languishing, sighing and nearly fainting beauty to my bosom, then fixing upon her humid lips a long, burning kiss, I nearly sucked her life away. Whilst occupied in this sweet employment, I unloosened the cord which kept my gown tight around me, and told her I then intended to reap the reward for the service I had rendered her.

The poor affrighted maid pleaded hard for a moment's pause and, weeping, strove to persuade me to spare her innocence—a token defense of virtue's laws. But I took her into my arms, and then began the soft contention preparatory to the fiercer fight. How delicious was the glow upon her beauteous neck and bare ivory shoulders, as I forced her on her back on the couch! With what voluptuous modesty did she hang her head as in the full tide of vigour I divided her swelling thighs. Quickly was the unspotted maid placed in that position which I did not permit her to rise from until she had forfeited every claim on that name. How luxuriously did her snowy hillocks rise against my bosom in wild confusion. Luckily she did not know what she was about to suffer. The confusion which seized her on my fingers again entering the cell of Venus for the purpose of introducing myself considerably favoured my proceedings. I felt the head of my weapon between her lips, and with a vigorous thrust strove to penetrate, but so cruelly tore her delicate little entrance that she screamed, tried to escape, and effectually threw me out. Inflamed with lechery and rage at this repulse, I swore by heaven if she again resisted I would convey her back to the tomb. Again I forcibly fixed myself between the lips of her yet untasted first fruits. I saw she was much alarmed at my rage and threats. It had a good effect: her fears lessened her defense. I then took every care to make my attack quite certain, and I began the fight of fierce delight, of pleasure mixed with pain. However enormous the disproportion between the place assailed and the attacking instrument, I soon found it piercing inward; her loud cries announced its victorious progress. Nothing now could appease my fury; the more she implored grace the more I pressed on with vigour. But never was conquest more difficult. Oh, how I was obliged to tear her up in forcing her virgin defenses! With what delicious tightness she clasped my rod of Aaron, as it entered the inmost recesses of her till then virgin sanctuary. How voluptuous was the heat of her young body! I was mad with enjoyment! Her young breasts rising and falling in wild confusion attracted my caresses. Guess my state of excitement. I sucked them, and at last bit them with delight. Although Julia was much overcome with her suffering, still she reproachfully turned her lovely eyes swimming with pain and languor on me. At this instant, with a final energetic thrust, I buried myself up to the very hair in her. A shriek proclaimed the change in her state; the ecstasy seized me and I shot into the inmost recesses of the womb of this innocent and beautiful child as copious a flood of burning sperm as ever was fermented under the cloak of a monk; whereupon, oh, marvellous effects of nature, the lovely Mezzia, spite of her cruel sufferings, ceded to my vigorous impressments. The pleasure overcame the pain, and the stretching of her ivory limbs, the quivering of her body, the eager clasping of her delicate arms, clearly spoke that nature's first effusion was distilling within her. When somewhat recovered from my ecstasy, without giving up possession of my prize, I lay on her soft bosom contemplating the numerous beauties fate had thrown into my possession. A profusion of dark brown tresses flowed negligently in luxurious curls to below her slender waist; under her fine-formed brows beamed the brightest eyes of ethereal blue ever created; her nose is Roman; her soft blushing cheeks imitate the rose; her teeth are like oriental pearls, whilst her yielding, pouting lips are most admirably turned. But at that moment these delicious inhalers of our fondest impressments were terribly wounded, so boisterous had been my enjoyment of them. Her face is decidedly Grecian, her bosom, shoulders, and neck resemble the purest ivory. On turning my eyes lower, on her young snowy hillocks, I blushed to see the crimson marks which my teeth had left on those lovely orbs. Softly insinuating my arms round her neck, I drew her blushing face to mine, and after impressing a few soft kisses on her yet bleeding lips, anxiously entreated the sweet girl to pardon my cruelty, assuring her with the tenderest oaths that I knew not what I was about, so much had the maddening transports overpowered me. She replied not. I placed one of her beautiful arms around my neck. She suffered it to remain. Again from her pouting lips did I inhale luxurious sweets.

Although I thought I had distilled my very existence into her, the life-inspiring suction completely reanimated my whole frame. I felt myself in as proud a state of erection within her as when I commenced her defloration; her young breasts heaving quickly, soft sighs, blushes and tremblings, sufficiently told that my prey also felt the return of my vigour. I determined the second enjoyment should amply repay her for all she had suffered, and began my movements with a caution and slowness which made her sigh with voluptuous ecstasy. It was now indeed that I leisurely enjoyed the lingering bliss, as by tender and ravishing degrees I forced myself up to the very quick within her. Scarcely mistress of her feelings, her yielding lips with delicious kisses joined more and more close to mine, blushes deeper and deeper covered her neck and blooming cheeks, her arms closely grasped me. By degrees my thrusts became quicker, but no complaint interrupted my joys. She panted with rapture; her limbs encircled me; she voluptuously heaved to my thrusts, whilst the wanton movements of her body and limbs, her ardent transports, her soft kisses, gave ample testimony of how quick the transition is from coy chastity to unrestrained luxurious enjoyment.

In short, I was as blessed as youth and voluptuous beauty could make me, until forced to retire from her arms to attend to my monastery duties. They were quickly dispatched, and after refreshing myself with a few hours' rest, I returned to my captive with recruited strength for the night's soft enjoyment. A smile of welcome was on her lovely countenance; she was dressed from a wardrobe I had pointed out to her, containing everything fit for her sex, with grateful pleasure I instantly perceived that her toilet had not been made for the mere purpose of covering her person, but every attention had been paid to setting off her numerous charms. The most care had been given to the disposing of her hair, whilst the lawn which covered her broad voluptuous breasts was so temptingly disposed that it was impossible to look upon her without burning desire. She sprang off the couch to meet me; for a moment I held her from me in an ecstasy of astonishment, then drawing her to my bosom, planted on her lips a kiss so long and so thrilling it was some moments ere we recovered from its effects. My passions were instantly in a blaze. I carried her to the side of the couch, placed her on it, and whilst sucking her delicious lips, uncovered her neck and breasts, then seizing her legs lifted them up, and threw up her clothes. A dissolving sentiment struggled with my more amorous desires. I stooped down to examine the voluptuous, glorious view. How luscious was the sight! Every part of her body was ivory whiteness, firmness and delicacy; the whole was perfect, everything charming; the white interspersed with small blue veins showed the transparency of the skin, whilst the darkness of the hair, softer than velvet, formed most beautiful shades, making a delicious contrast with the vermilion lips of her new-stretched love sheath, the brilliant vermilion of the shell evidently heightened with the blood of her defunct virginity. Tired of admiring without enjoyment, I carried my mouth and hand to everything before me, until I could no longer bear myself. Raising myself from my stooping position, I extended her thighs to the utmost, and placed myself standing between them, then letting loose my rod of Aaron, which was no sooner at liberty but it flew up with the same impetuosity with which a tree straightens itself when the cord that keeps it bent towards the ground comes to be cut, with my right hand I directed it towards the pouting slit so that the head was soon in. Laying myself down on her, I drew her lips to mine; again I thrust, I entered. Another thrust buried it deeper; she closed her eyes, but tenderly squeezed me to her bosom; again I pushed; her soft lips rewarded me. Another shove caused her to sigh deliciously—another push made our junction complete. I scarcely knew what I was about; everything now was in active exertion—tongues, lips, bellies, arms, thighs, legs, bottoms, every part in voluptuous motion until our spirits completely abandoned every part of our bodies to convey themselves into the place where pleasures reigned with so furious but still with so delicious a sentiment. I dissolved myself into her at the very moment nature had caused her to give down her tribute to the intoxicating joy. My lovely prey soon came to herself, but it was only to invite me by her numberless charms to plunge her into the same condition. She passed her arms round my neck and sucked my lips with dovelike kisses. I opened my eyes and fixed them on hers; they were filled with dissolving languor; I moved within her, her eyes closed instantly. The tender squeeze of her love sheath round my instrument satisfied me as to the state she was in. Again I thrust. 'Ah!' she sighed, 'the pleasure suffocates me.' I thrust furiously; her limbs gradually stiffened, she gave one more movement in response to the fierce thrusts made into her organ; we both discharged together.

It will be no use, Angelo, to give you any further description of my enjoyment of this adorable child, but the agonising reflection that I must part with my delicious prize nearly drives me to distraction. During cooler moments I have explained to her the necessity of a separation, and pointed out to her the danger of her remaining in this country. The solemn assurance I have given her of her safety from the fangs of the church has tendered to comfort her. But then, Angelo, how can I force myself to part with so voluptuous a creature? Advise and counsel your friend.

PEDRO

# Letter 15

Angelo to Pedro


Holy St Peter, spare me! What in the name of Beelzebub has taken possession of you? How can you force yourself to part with this voluptuous creature? How did your reverence contrive to force yourself from the arms of Camilla, Rosa St Peter, the poor fisherman's daughter Bianca, and the half a dozen other young beauties whom I have conveyed over the sea to the great gratification of the Turks in Algiers and Tunis, but to the much greater gratification of ourselves, by well lining our own pockets with African gold? Write to me again in about a fortnight; let me know if the fever is still hot upon you. I guess about that time you will be somewhat cooler; at all events a month is the utmost time I can afford you for your amusement with your new-found charmer. In six weeks I shall be ready to depart with the cartel for Algiers. You know that under our agreement I ought to have at least a fortnight's enjoyment of the girl on shore. The time spent on the voyage to Algiers is so very short that these young creatures, from sickness, very rarely afford me any pleasure. I wish you could contrive to get a pure maid or two for the Dey of Algiers. I could get almost any price for one, so fond is he of cutting off maidenheads. But I forget myself, you are equally as bad as the Dey himself in that respect, so I must try to procure one myself. Let me know at your earliest leisure when I may expect the young Mezzia.

# Letter 16

Pedro to Angelo


You are correct in your observation, Angelo—uncontrolled possession, in time, surely abates the fiercest passions. It is now three weeks since I relieved the youthful Mezzia of her virginity, every subsequent night having been passed in her delicious arms, the novelty of her beauties begins I find to lose its invigorating effect. But still, Angelo, I dread the arrival of the day I must part with her. She has been particularly inquisitive as to where she is to be sent. I have pacified her by stating she is going to Ireland, part of the kingdom of Great Britain, where the great mass of the population are Catholic. When she heard they were Catholic her fears at first resumed their sway, but were removed when she was solemnly assured that it was out of the power of the clergy there to contemn or punish anyone, convents and incarceration of females being no part of the law of that kingdom.


This day week is appointed for our separation. She has begun to amuse herself by sorting the clothes I have given her in trunks previous to her departure. I have been extremely liberal in my gifts, particularly in the old jewels and ornaments which you know have served for the same purpose so many times. She is very lovely, Angelo, and will fetch a magnificent price, maid or no maid. I suppose it would be of no use attempting to pass her off at Algiers as a virgin? I am afraid the eunuchs belonging to the Dey's seraglio are too well experienced in these matters. Farewell. But I forgot I have informed her that she will be consigned to my sister, the Lady Abbess at the Convent of St Theresa. So you must for a few hours assume your old disguise of the abbess, which will deliver her to your enjoyment without trouble. May the saint you most approve of have you in his holy keeping.

PEDRO

# Letter 17

## Angelo to Pedro

I do not wonder at your regret at parting with the young, beautiful Mezzia. She is indeed a bijou. Happy Pedro! Indeed I envy you the joys supreme—joys you must have tasted in her arms when with amorous fury you plucked the virgin rose. She arrived here in safety. I had her conveyed unseen into our unknown and private retreat. Of course I assumed the disguise of the lady abbess, your sister, which I think I acted extremely well. The poor innocent had no suspicion of the deception, although the kiss I gave her in receiving her from your messenger was warm enough. I gave her to understand that I was aware of her escape from the tomb, but made not the least hint of any knowledge as to what had passed between you. She appeared extremely low and dejected. I did everything to comfort her. But I must leave off until tomorrow, when you shall hear how I get on with her. After supper I told her, as it was a very lonely part of the convent, we would pass the night together, but that for a short time I should leave her to get the key of the convent from the porter sister; during my absence she might get into bed, which, you know, is quite large enough for two. In seven or eight minutes I returned with a key in my hand, which I laid on the table. She was nearly undressed. I sat down pretending to read a missal, but in fact was wandering over the numerous charms she disclosed at every turn to my ardent (but to her unseen) gaze. At last she got into bed, upon which I drew the curtains and got undressed myself. This I despatched as well as the awkwardness of the dress would let me, and having put on a proper female nightdress, I got into bed, intending to lie still until she was asleep, and then to make myself master of her person whilst she was unconscious of what I was about. But accident gave her up to my enjoyment sooner than I expected.

You may suppose the state I was in, placed by the side of such a delicious creature. In fact I was in the most fierce erection possible when, in turning herself, the unsuspecting girl placed her hand upon my throbbing instrument. You had too well cultivated her to leave her in doubt as to what she had felt. A faint scream satisfied me as to the discovery. It was no use to carry on the deception further with her. I therefore seized her in my arms and stopped her cries with my kisses; in fact she screamed so loud at being suddenly grasped by me that I was almost afraid she might be heard by someone. I quickly reminded her of how much depended on her silence—her life might be the forfeit of her folly, you may rely upon it that whilst trying to quiet her screams I was not otherwise idle. I threw myself on her—her thighs were quickly divided. Her cries subsided but tears flowed. I gave her very little time to reflect whether it was best to alarm the convent, or to suffer in peace. It was not more than fourteen or fifteen seconds from the time of her discovering my sex ere what she had laid her hand on was safely lodged to its full extent in its natural receiver. There can be no doubt she gained by its discovery. How magical is the influence of the distinction of our sex over the feelings of the softer one. Shrieks, cries, tears and resistance accompanied the discovery and my seizing of her, but directly she felt its head dividing her lips of life her resistance ceased, and her cries became hushed; as it penetrated her tears became dried; but when it pierced her up to the quick, soft exclamations, tremulous sighs and a general trembling of the limbs and body only accompanied our complete junction. Nature had already assumed its sway—a few rapid thrusts gave a fillip to pleasure and as my movements became quicker, so did the seduction overpower the little remains of modesty you had left her. In short, she quickly received as

much pleasure as she bestowed, if I may judge from the sweetness of her kisses, the ardency of her pressures, with a thousand
other little etceteras which cannot be described and are only
felt in the high enjoyment. In short, so mutually had the ecstasy
operated on us that the dissolving moment seized us at the same
time. Oh, Pedro, how ecstatic was her joy as the essence of life
was shot up to her vitals! Her delicate arms closely encircled
my body, her legs were crossed over my loins holding me as
strongly as if grasped by a vice, nor did she loosen her hold until she had extracted the very last drop from me. Then the gradual unclasping of her arms and legs, the conclusive stretching
of her body, the delicious trembling shudder, all feelingly spoke
how much her senses had been gratified. This was indeed a
night of joy for me! I had for a month refrained from sexual in-
tercourse and consequently was in a state to give as well as taste
myself the most luxurious transports. If beauty is necessary to
renew the vigour after repeated enjoyment, Mezzia possesses
every charm to excite the desires enjoyment has cooled. We did
not close our eyes during the night, which was spent in a continued round of varied pleasure of the most delicious nature.
The sun had risen in the east ere Morpheus placed his heavy finger on our eyelids.


She has asked me the reason for your deceiving her about
your sister. I put the best face on it, and informed her it arose
from your wish not to alarm her by letting her know she was to
be consigned to a friar. I also gave her to understand that I was
perfectly acquainted with all that had passed between you and
her, and as an excuse for myself boldly told her it was utterly
impossible to resist the temptation thrown in my way by fortune
of making myself as happy with her as you had been. I only
regretted that the time she was doomed to be mine was so short.
After three or four days passed with her she became extremely
curious in her enquiries as to what kind of place Ireland was.

I parried her enquiries by informing her that so much had her charms affected me that I had determined to abandon Italy altogether, and should marry her when we arrived in Ireland (when we do, perhaps I may). The child believed me. Indeed her charms do provoke me exceedingly.

Although every night is spent in her soft embraces, there is not a day passes but I gratify my senses of seeing, feeling and enjoying her with every excitement the sight and touch are capable of giving. In fact I do not recollect a female who had the power of so strongly exciting my passions, nor do I think I ever enjoyed a girl with half the assiduity or rapidity I have her. I consider her superior in her motions to any woman I ever enjoyed, and the heat and tightness of her love sheath give an indescribable voluptuousness to the rapture. Adieu, Pedro. If I do not write to you again before I sail for Algiers, you may not expect to hear from me until I return.

ANGELO

# Letter 18

Emily Barlow to Maria Williams

London, 8 May 1816


Dearest Maria—

You requested me in your last letter to write you an account of my life while at Algiers. I thought I could not do better than send you a copy of my letter to Sylvia Carey. I have also sent with them a parcel of letters belonging to Father Angelo, a Roman Catholic priest, who left them by accident on board Abdallah's ship while at Toulon. This priest was employed by the Dey in concert with Abdallah to secure my friend Sylvia, as you will see by the Dey's letter to Abdallah.


I will now continue my history from the time that I received Sylvia's last letter. I had been with child about six months, when the Dey's neglect assured me some fresh worthy engaged his amorous moments. A rumour ran that it was a countrywoman of mine. The Dey was immovable; neither myself nor any of my companions could get the secret out of him, until one day the chief eunuch told me in a confidential manner that if I chose I could see my rival. Although I hated her in my heart for robbing me of that which was dear to me, my curiosity got the better of my feelings, and I accepted his offer. He led me through several rooms I had never been in before, until we came to a large chamber parted in the middle by a curtain. My guide motioned me to look as he drew the curtain apart. The first object that met my eyes was a naked female leaning on a couch, face downward, and the Dey with his noble shaft plunged up to the hilt in her. At this moment the Dey turned his head and discovered me. Surprise nailed me to the spot. He clasped his hands around his lady, raised her from the recumbent position, still keeping his weapon in her, wheeled round and brought her full to my view. Imagine to yourself, dearest Maria, what must have been my emotions on my beholding in his arms my friend Sylvia, she who had added to my anxiety by her unfeeling letter. I uttered a hurried exclamation and fainted.

On my recovery I found myself in bed and Sylvia bending over me. 'Forgive me, dearest Emily,' she exclaimed, 'for the harsh letter I wrote you. Little did I then think that I too should fall a sacrifice to the dear wicked Dey. I now wonder how you could have so eloquently described the very things that have occurred to me. But compose yourself, my dear, the Dey has forbid me giving you any account of myself, as he wishes to narrate it himself.'

The next day I was sitting on the sofa when the Dey entered my apartment. I tried to frown on him, but could not, for he drew his robe on one side and disclosed that delightful instrument that attunes my heart to harmony. I threw myself on my back, and in a moment his highness was in the pinnacle of bliss. Thrice did he return my embraces ere he withdrew; then, seating himself beside me on the couch, he began as follows.

'You no doubt are dying with curiosity to know how your friend came into my possession, but what a silly child you must have been to suppose that I would have permitted you to write letters and receive answers without myself knowing the contents. I had a hearty laugh over what you told your friend, and I assure you I equally enjoyed the answer you received from her, but was determined to pay the minx for calling me a beast if it lay in my power. You recollect she stated she was at Toulon. One of my ships was about to sail for that port. I sent for Captain Abdallah and offered him a liberal reward to abduct the young lady. He found little difficulty in effecting his purpose, and about a month since he returned with this coy lady to Algiers. Whilst he was gone I was much puzzled how I should proceed with her. After canvassing twenty different modes of subduing her to my pleasure, I determined on the following as the most likely to add to my gratification in debauching her. I determined on her arrival to represent a French physician, and make her fly into my arms in that character to avoid me in my real one.

'In pursuance of this scheme I fitted up the slave driver's house at the bottom of the palace gardens in every way proper to represent the house of a medical man of some eminence. For a purpose which I shall by and by explain I caused to be made in the principal sitting-room a secret recess or cupboard, so well contrived that no one could discover it, although at the same time those inside could see and hear quite plainly everything passing in the room. My arrangements were quite finished before she arrived. I had an interview with Abdallah prior to her being brought on shore. When he had received his instructions for his little part in the drama of deception, his description of her gratified me much. I longed for the moment to arrive when her naked beauties were to be offered to my inspection.

'If there is anything that tends to the subjection of a haughty woman, it is the attacking of her modesty at once in the most sensible part. Nothing tends to humble coy chastity so much as our system of the slave market where captives are exposed, naked, and left unreservedly to the sight and feel of whoever chooses to bid for them. The most stubborn beauty will in time inevitably fall under its subduing influence. Next morning she was brought on shore and placed in one of the slave bazaars, under the direction of Abdallah. She was stripped entirely naked, then a silk cloak was given her to wrap herself in, until my eunuch came to examine whether she was worthy of being sent to my serail, as I had first choice. This Abdallah informed her of in her own language. You may guess her state of alarm. In the course of the morning one of my eunuchs, attended by four black slaves, went to the bazaar in state. Abdallah requested her to throw off her cloak; this she refused to do; consequently they were obliged to take it from her by force, as they were also obliged to lay her on her back on a couch so that the eunuch might examine her properly as to her virginity. The four slaves with difficulty held her down whilst the eunuch performed his duty.

'She struggled and screamed without intermission whilst Hassan, the eunuch, made his survey. When he had finished he asked Abdallah, in French, what was demanded for her; he answered (in the same language), twelve purses. Hassan replied that he doubted whether she was a virgin, and that he did not think she would suit the Dey. "But," asked he, "of what country is she?"'

'On being informed she was English, "Oh," he replied, "the Dey has sworn never to have another Englishwoman, since he was obliged to strangle Zulima a few days ago." Theodora (the name I had ordered for her), who understood perfectly every word that was spoken, on hearing of your supposed death, forgot her own troubles and feinted. By proper remedies she was quickly restored to her senses, but every precaution was taken to make her believe no one cared about her swooning.

Hassan refused to purchase her and left the bazaar. This farce was repeated by several of my eunuchs during the day, some objecting to the price, some finding fault with her person—all declining to purchase her, but all examining her and feeling her parts as to her fitness for the station she was doomed to be placed in. It was evident to Abdallah that she began to submit to her destiny, she plainly saw, however it might outrage her modesty, there was no evading the examinations which were scrupulously attended to in that most secret part for which to be touched by man is nearly a death blow to chastity. Of course, I did not permit her to be seen by anyone but my own slaves, in various disguises; all the while the poor girl thought she was in the public market for sale.

'Abdallah now, in her own language, began to abuse her for want of attraction in not finding a quick sale. This was the moment appointed for the performance of my part of the play. I accordingly entered the room like the others, and made her undergo the necessary examinations, first feeling her beautiful ivory breasts, then slipping my hand down over her smooth satin belly till, descending, my fingers mixed with the soft down which covered and beautifully shaded her grotto of love.

'The poor girl I thought would have sunk to the ground whilst undergoing this touching ceremony—indeed she would have had I not supported her; but I proceeded in my search, heedless of her tears. Softly I seized on the delicious lips of her virgin opening, and forced my forefinger half in. I finished my search and asked Abdallah her price. He treated me as if I had been a person of no consequence, and lowered his demand from twelve to eight purses. I bid him seven purses for her, which he refused to take. I told him I could not afford to give more, and then enquired what country she came from. He then informed me from France, at which, pretending to be much astonished, I asked her in French (in which we had been talking all along) whether she had understood what we said if she was a French-woman? As well as her feeling would permit her, she answered in good French that she was English. Nearly choked with tears, she informed me of the manner in which she had been torn from her friends, and submissively entreated me to give the price demanded for her, assuring me I should have it and much more for ransom. I pretended to take great interest in what she said; asked her many questions as to the rank and property of her friends, which she represented, there is no doubt, in their true light. On my expressing doubts if I should get the sum back if I bought her, she assured me over and over again there was no occasion to have the least mistrust, and again and again piteous-ly entreated me to save her from further shame. I at last pretend-ed to be overcome by her tears and supplications and therefore told Abdallah he should have his demand. He appeared quite glad to get rid of her. Under the pretence of ordering a palan-quin to convey her to my home, and purchasing some dresses, I went out. Whilst I was absent Abdallah informed her I was a Frenchman, and first physician in Algiers, also deputy consul for that nation, and that she could not have fallen into better hands. On returning I observed with pleasure a considerable al-teration for the better in her looks. When she had attired herself in the robes and veil I had brought her, she was conducted to the palanquin, and the maid was soon in the house at the bottom of the garden.

The large room had been fitted up in a very handsome style, suitable to a man of my supposed rank. Among the neces-saries, you may suppose convenient couches were not omitted. Adjoining was a smaller room, only partitioned off by a fine silk curtain; this was arranged for sleeping or (more properly speaking) for the purpose of enjoyment. In introducing her to the boudoir I plainly felt the hand of Theodora tremble; no doubt the appearance of the place strongly indicated its use. However, I took no notice of her fears, but told her at present they were the apartments she was to occupy. I pointed out to her where she would find every article of dress, and also informed her I would send one of my women to attend and help her at her toilet, as she might be in some difficulty as to how the garments were worn. She timidly asked me what I meant by one of my women. I explained to her the custom of the country—that it was usual to have as many women here as we could support, who were bought in the same manner as I had purchased her, that I had two slaves of the kind, one of whom should attend and assist her; that it was impossible for me to marry a Mahometan, being myself a Protestant Christian. She looked at me fearfully, and said she hoped no advantage would be taken of her unhappy condition and waited with breathless anxiety my answer. I approached her, and taking one of her hands in mine and encircling her waist with the other, solemnly assured her that her modesty or virtue had nothing to fear from me. "I have bought you for the purpose of returning you to your country and friends, and by this kiss of friendship," said I, drawing her soft lips to mine, "you have nothing to fear." She blushingly submitted her lips to my pressure. I did not encroach upon her good nature, but requested she would make herself as happy as possible and assured her that no time should be lost in communicating with her friends.

'I left her and sent a handsome Circassian girl to assist her in dressing. As the slave could not speak a word except in her native language, there was no fear of her betraying who I was. I told her what she was to do, and to return when she had finished. In about an hour the slave came back, and I returned to the apartment of Theodora. I was indeed struck by the blaze of beauty she exhibited when dressed after our fashion, her coal-black hair, beautifully parted over her noble ivory forehead, peeping out from beneath her headdress. "My God," I cried, "how is it possible the chief eunuch of the Dey could have passed over charms such as you possess?" The name of the Dey brought the recollection of him to her, and she dropped on a couch overcome by her feelings. She entreated me with tears not to name the Dey again to her. Of course, I promised to comply with her wishes, but demanded how it was the name of the Dey affected her so much, a person she could know nothing of. "Ah," she replied, "I know more of him than you are aware, of." On my expressing my surprise and incredulity, she was induced to enter into the history of your falling into my hands. Every now and then I interrupted her revelations with expressions of astonishment, but she did not mention the last letter she had written to you. Then she related what she had heard between Abdallah and Hassan in the morning, and enquired whether I believed there was any truth in it. I assured her it was impossible to tell, but such things the Dey was particular in. It was nothing to him to order a female to be strangled in consequence of the slightest offence. The poor girl was much affected at my corroboration of Hassan's assertion. My respectful behaviour was evidently every moment establishing me in her confidence. After we had dined I informed her that the greater part of the morning was devoted to attending my patients, but tomorrow afternoon should be spent in preparing the necessary correspondence with her friends in France. Towards the evening I asked her if she would walk in the garden towards the sea. I had taken care to give very particular orders that no one should be permitted in there, or on the sea beach at the back of the harem. She took hold of my arm during our walk, and seemed to gain courage and spirits as her fears evidently decreased at my seeming respect. After walking until we were tired, we returned to the house—

A blushing lovely maid she entered it,

But ere she left was quite another thing.


'I did not accompany her to her apartments, but took leave below, respectfully kissing her hand, and assuring her that on the morrow I would get back from my professional pursuits as early as possible, and the remainder of the day should be devoted to her service. She little dreamt of the service I meant.


'I had selected a slave to attend on her who spoke French, so there was no difficulty as to anything she might want. Next day, in the afternoon, on being announced to her I found her comparatively easy in her mind. After the usual compliments I proceeded to business. The writing materials were brought and we set to work opposite the window which commanded a view of the garden and the long walk but left us entirely screened ourselves. Whilst busy on the letter, on a signal given by one of my attendants, which was merely the imitation of the chirping of a bird, I pretended to look accidentally out of the window, and started up with astonishment, saying, "What can he want here?" Getting up so suddenly alarmed Theodora, who with horror instantly recognised Hassan coming up the long walk. "My God," said I aloud to myself, without paying any attention to her, but alive to her state of mind. Her fears immediately acted just as I wished. She sprang forward and clung round my neck, saying, "Oh, save me, save me! It is me he wants; I fear it; I feel it. Oh, in the name of God save me." "I dare not—my life, everything is at stake," I replied. "But stop, perhaps you are alarmed without cause." I rang the bell. The servant who answered was directed to meet Hassan, and if he asked for me to say I was gone to my country house with a female slave. The papers were quickly carried to the private recess ready provided, in which we also hid ourselves. We had not been concealed long ere a considerable noise was heard between Hassan and my servant. Presently they both entered the room wrangling. The servant said, '"You see, he is not here." Hassan replied, "But my orders are peremptory. I am to search for the English slave and bring her to the Dey's harem. I have nearly lost my life for not purchasing her yesterday."

'Here Theodora had sunk on my bosom; it was only with the greatest difficulty I could stop her sobs. But there was no fear of Hassan hearing her, even had she made more noise than she did. However, I took the opportunity of closing her mouth with my lips, softly encouraging her not to give way to her fears, assuring her she would be protected at the risk of my life. Hassan proceeded to search the sleeping apartments, but did not find what he sought. He told my servant that he must proceed after me to my country seat, for his life depended on his success. When he was gone we emerged from our confinement. It was now necessary something should be done. To escape from Algiers was utterly impossible. In the course of five or six hours Hassan would surely return. For some time I appeared utterly lost. How to act I knew not. She still clung to me, bathing me with tears, entreating me to kill her rather than deliver her up to the cruel Dey. Time rapidly slipped away—three hours had already passed—nothing decided on. Every moment her despair was growing stronger. She was in my arms, her head resting on my bosom, my waistcoat moistened with her tears. Suddenly, starting up, I summoned the attendant and demanded if he was a true believer. He replied he was. "Is it written," said I anxiously, "in your Koran, and expressly forbidden by Mahomet, that no true believer should meddle with the wife of another, whether

Mussulman or otherwise?" It was his reply, "So has the Prophet written." "Fetch me a Koran." It was brought. The attendant pointed out a verse which I pretended to translate to her. "It is your only chance of escape," I cried. "Become my wife and you escape pollution, and perhaps something more; there is no other way of avoiding the tyrant." Her fears of the Dey quickly decided her fate; she consented.

'I instantly pretended to write a letter to the Protestant minister of the English consul's family, which we both signed—I told her he would not attend unless we both requested it. Everything had been fully prepared. She saw me direct the letter to the English Consul. Everything tended to lull her into security, in about an hour more Ben Izacks, the English Jew diamond merchant whom I had directed to perfect himself in the part of an English priest for the completion of my scheme, arrived with all the assurance of his sect, cleverly disguised to perform the ceremony. The ring was ready, the contract made out, when my bride requested to speak a few words to the clergyman in private. I immediately withdrew with the witnesses who were of course my own slaves, in a few minutes I was summoned by the Jew. I afterwards learned from him that the only question she asked of him was whether he was certain I was a Christian. You may suppose he perfectly satisfied her on that point. Without further delay the ceremony proceeded. Izacks performed his part with proper solemnity. She had just sufficient strength left to pronounce the mystic oath, and at the very instant the ceremony was finished she sank fainting in my arms, unable longer to support the flurry and disorder of her feelings. I instantly dismissed Izacks and the attendants. Alone I supported her into the boudoir, where I intended the consummation should directly take place.

'Assuming now the privileges of a husband, I placed her on the couch, and tenderly clasping her to my bosom soon reaped a rich harvest of soft thrilling kisses. With a trembling sigh the languishing maid opened her heavenly black eyes, but unable to bear my gaze quickly shut them again. I now boldly explained to her the absolute and immediate necessity of her resigning to me the blessing I was entitled to in the enjoyment of her person, for in this country a marriage is a nullity until the husband has consummated it. Should the wretch Hassan return and find we had omitted any part of the ceremony, instant advantage would be taken of it, therefore all we had done would be of no use. Whilst I was thus explaining myself, I was also busily unbuttoning the bodice which covered the beauties of her bosom, every now and then placing on her soft rosy lips the most delicious kisses. She but feebly resisted. How shall I describe her delightful confusion when my hand boldly slid over her panting globes? It is impossible; words cannot do justice to the situation. Although I was using the absolute authority of a husband over her you will recollect that her submission to my proceedings was entirely from fear created by the dread of myself, only in another shape. Ours was not a union of love, but one hastily submitted to by her to save herself from the embraces of an imaginary brutal monster created by her fears and false information alone. Under such circumstances there could of course be very little love on her side, although there might be some little respect for the service I had rendered her—in the supposed risk I was running in offending the Dey by marrying her. Thus, although she had no pretext left on which to oppose every liberty I now took with her beautiful person, still I could plainly see, as I was divesting her voluptuous body of its coverings, how dreadful was the shock her modesty sustained in being obliged to resign herself even to a husband. Modesty may struggle, but it very seldom struggles successfully with me. It was evident from her agitation that her bashfulness would have struggled against my proceedings had she not been fettered by the oath of obedience she had just sworn on the altar of God. If she had even found out the deception which had been practised on her, any opposition would have now been fruitless. Her hour of instruction was arrived. I had determined she should receive her lesson. Although not assisted by any tie on her affections, I of course was perfectly aware how quick is the influence of pleasure on the softer sex. If the land is properly cultivated, it will always produce its crops. So it is with lovely women. Rid them of their virginity, enjoy them properly, and it is wonderful to observe the rapidity with which the seed of pleasure will thrive and yield a rich harvest to the happy cultivator. You may guess I was not long preparing myself or my trembling victim for the mighty business. Clasping my lovely beauty in my arms I easily laid her on the cushion and myself by her side. Her swelling snowy breasts heaved with her laboured breathing, with one arm round her neck, the other hand unresistedly traversed all her beauties, until suddenly forcing my hand between her smooth, polished thighs, I took possession of the port of love. Her tremblings, her sighs, increased rapidly; with bashful modesty she entreated, she prayed me to remove my hand. I promised everything for a kiss. However, the kiss taken, I did not keep my word. My reasons were good. It had not been agreed whether it should be given or taken. By dint of bargaining we agreed on a second, which was to be received by me. Then with my unoccupied hand guiding her trembling delicate arms around my neck, and leaning over her to receive it, the soft, thrilling, delicious kiss was not only received, but perfectly given, in such a manner that love could not have done it better. So much good faith deserved to be rewarded. I immediately withdrew my hand, but I do not know by what accident one of my knees occupied the place I had just vacated. A soft struggle ensued, during which half-breathed words and sighs escaped her—every now and then, "Ah", and "you must not", "pray do not", and so on until I had securely placed myself between her soft swelling thighs. This effected, I found not the smallest difficulty in stretching them at pleasure to their utmost spread. Shame and surprise had now quite overpowered my charming, panting, blushing prize.

'I was not very eager or in great haste to finish my task. I delight in delays when I am certain of coming to the end of the journey. I clearly saw, in spite of her modesty, that my kisses and touches had considerably inflamed her senses, so seizing her left hand with my right, with gentle force I conducted it to the key which I told her was to open the road to the sweetest enjoyments. I entreated her to take it in her hand. She did not reply, but requested me to spare her modesty. "In the name of God," she cried, "have pity on me." Her tears began to flow, but they only added to her beauty, and inflamed me more strongly, so pretending to be much astonished, I reminded her that she was on the conjugal bed, and therefore it was necessary to our common pleasure she should not now show any opposition to my wishes. But it was of no use; she would not be persuaded to take it in her hand. During this contention my member had become furious, and was beating his head against the lips of the port shortly doomed to receive it.

'Finding her modesty was not to be overcome on this point, I desisted, and taking my instrument in my hand, placed the head between the lips and with my finger and thumb contrived to stretch the delicate little opening sufficiently wide to insert the head entirely. As the moment of her martyrdom approached, so by degrees did her confusion and agitation increase. The insertion of the head of my stiff virgin-stretcher caused her delicious ivory breasts to beat against my bosom with the rapidity of lightning, whilst her milk-white neck and shoulders were covered with burning blushes. She would have spoken, but could not give utterance to the words. However, talking just then was of no great consequence, so making a furious thrust I strove to penetrate her virgin sanctuary, but the avenue was too tight to give way to a first attempt. A second thrust, made with circumspection, was a little more successful; a third and fourth deepened my penetration; at last, as I followed up my success with strength and rapidity, the sweet obstacle began to give way, until I had pierced myself halfway into her. How delicious were the varying expressions which her sweet countenance now exhibited. When she first felt the penetration her confusion was so great she could not keep her eyes open, but as ground was gained the confusion began to dissipate, her eyes lost their unconsciousness, astonishment mixed with pain became clearly marked on her lovely countenance and soft cries began to find vent in spite of my fierce kisses. I now made a desperate effort to break through the remaining defenses of her coy chastity, but was prevented by the ecstasy seizing me; the seed of life distilled from me like a deluge.

'This stopped my proceedings for some moments, but did not force me to withdraw from her. In fact, though I quite overflowed the part penetrated, still very little of my stiffness or vigour was lost. Her soft lips, the nipples of her well-formed breasts, soon renewed my strength. During the cessation of hostilities she entreated me, if I loved her, to withdraw my furious instrument. "You will kill me," she cried in a most piteous voice. "I certainly shall die; it is impossible to sustain your cruel tearing." "If I love you? Can you doubt it? Have I not risked my life for you?" replied I, tenderly sucking her lips, and thrusting my tongue into her mouth. "No doubt, delicious love, the pain you suffer is cruel, but it is entailed upon your sex and it will quickly subside; nor can you participate in the soft joys of love without undergoing the ordeal; therefore, dear maid, submit with courage, the most voluptuous joys will be your reward." At this moment I began to pierce again with all my force; the overflowing of my seed within her considerably assisted, having oiled the road so much that I felt myself gradually stretching her, but still it must have hurt her dreadfully, as her loud cries testified. Pity for her sufferings caused me to stop a moment, to assure her that it was nearly over. "Feel," I cried, "my sweet life, it is nearly all entered." Agitation with her sufferings, or fear of further anguish, I know not which, induced her to obey. She found the truth of my assertion, my instrument was three parts within her, but there it stuck as if it were too thick to enter further. Whilst her hand was upon it, I made a furious effort—again it penetrated. "Ah!" she cried, "stay your cruel thrusts, you murder me!" but collecting all my strength, and making one tremendous lunge, I sent it gloriously and triumphantly into her to the utmost length. The couch which was the field of battle trembled under the shock. You may judge of my vigour for the very curtains of the apartment shook In vain she entreated me to withdraw the arrow which was pierced up to her very entrails.

'"No," I replied, "it is now all over; you have nothing further to apprehend; from a pure virgin you have become a chaste wife and all that remains to be done is to make the travelling easy to me and pleasurable to you. This, sweet love, can only be effected by judicious and frequent enjoyments. Believe me, from the moment the close union of our bodies proclaimed your maidenhead taken, your sufferings must become less and less acute." My words were supported by actions. Master of the citadel, I assumed all the conqueror's rights. Drawing myself nearly out of her, with one vigorous thrust I plunged back Again and again was the experiment repeated. Her tears flowed, intermixed with cries, sobs and sighs. I desisted not, but whispered, "Courage, courage, my dear love, soon you will feel the softest pleasure." At every fresh thrust the difficulty of entry decreased. Now lost in ravishment indefinable, I grasped her strongly in my arms, and thrust with fury and without care.

'Her cries had subsided. The ecstatic moment again approaching, I drove myself up to the very hilt; it was impossible to enjoy a more voluptuous conjunction, a copious discharge filled the recesses of her womb; her virginity was gone. I sank insensible in her arms, entirely overcome with the most delicious the most perfect of all earthly enjoyments.

'On recovering my senses I was still buried securely in my lovely Theodora; her head was reclining on her right shoulder; with gentle respiration her ivory breasts deliriously heaved against my bosom; her eyes were closed, but the pearly dew still glistened in her dark silken eyelashes. Tenderly encircling her neck with my arms, I kissed off the trembling drops. How exquisite was the gratification of my senses at this moment! Still trembling with the ecstasy of having deflowered as pure and lovely a virgin as ever was stretched on the altar of Venus, how thrilling was the joy when I again drew her soft lips to mine, feeding my senses with the luxurious inhalement of her balmy breath, amidst a shower of dove-like kisses! One of her arms, which lay by my side, I gently placed around my neck. She withdrew it not. Gradually her lovely eyes opened and although I could clearly read in their dissolving expression how great was the pain she felt from the enormous machine buried within her, but still with joy I saw by the expression of her eyes that complete possession of her lovely body had reared the bud of tenderness in the senses of my victim. Although at present its blossom was a painful one, the sweetness of her kisses, the voluptuous heaving of her breasts, that indescribable look which true modesty surely shows at the moment it has received its irreparable shock from powerful man, all tended quickly to renew the vigour I had lost in unloosening her virgin zone. The burning blushes which with rapidity covered her neck and shoulders, the increasing heaving of her breasts, the trembling of her limbs and body, all proclaimed the distention she internally felt, caused by her external beauties. To be in this state and be quiet between the swelling thighs of such a beauty was impossible. I gradually withdrew myself nearly out of her. A loud sigh followed my motion—then in like gradual manner I sheathed myself up to the hair—but again on our close junction a cry escaped her. "Idol of my soul," I cried, "does it hurt you? Fear not; bear up but a short time; your sufferings will cease forever." "Indeed, dear sir," she sobbed, "you hurt me cruelly. I shall die—pray spare me." Again I slowly and gradually withdrew myself and returned my instrument into its delicious sheath; but, instead of driving it up to the hilt until our hair mixed as before, when it was all but an inch and a half in I stopped. Finding the insertion accompanied by a deep sigh only, again and again I repeated the movement, tremulous agitation being the only response. Satisfied as I was that this manner of enjoying her did not hurt her much, still it was impossible to continue it long. The enjoyment of her was too exciting to permit me to have complete command of my feelings from the beginning to the end of enjoyment, consequently her beauties soon worked me up into a fury, an agony of delight, my thrusts keeping pace and becoming fiercer as the excitement increased. The strength of my furious shocks made everything around us tremble by their violence. In the intervals between lunges, as I withdrew myself from her, she renewed her painful cries, loudly vociferating, "Oh, pray, sir, spare me—for heaven's sake stop. I cannot bear it—indeed you tear me to pieces—cruel. Ah! oh, I shall die." Then, "Oh, my God." Then again (her voice subduing into softer supplication), "Oh, dear sir, for pity's sake spare me! dear sir, pray forbear." I murmured it was impossible to desist, I could only stop her complaints by closing her mouth with kisses. She saw from my agitation it was in vain to supplicate, so became resigned to her fate. No doubt she felt some consolation as every moment lessened the pain; sighs began to usurp the place of cries and when she withdrew her lips from mine it was only to regain the breath I had nearly sucked away. At this moment I plainly saw that her nature was touched by my energetic proceedings. The ecstasy again seized me, and for the third time I dissolved myself away within her.

'Thus did I consummate my marriage, and thus did the tender girl forfeit her virginity for her prudery in attacking your feelings. It is true the Rubicon was now passed with her, but I had made up my mind not to undeceive her as to who possessed her maidenhead until she had enjoyed the soft pleasures of coition sufficiently to reward her for the loss, and to make the discovery a matter of no great consequence. Twice more thereafter (making five in the whole) did I make play and force the defunct maid to sustain the assault, each time piercing her up to the quick with the most redoubtable and lively thrusts, and bedewing her burning receiver with the dew of life; then thinking I had effected sufficient for her first instruction, I got up for the purpose of meeting Hassan on his return (as I assured her) but desired she would not disturb herself. After a few more caresses I resigned her to the God of sleep, the only arms but my own or a female's I intend she shall ever repose in.

'Hassan came at the appointed time. Theodora had fallen into a refreshing slumber, out of which I was obliged to disturb her, but desired her not to be alarmed, assuring her no one should injure her. I explained as quickly as possible that the Dey's eunuch was not satisfied with the assertion that our marriage had been consummated, which rendered it necessary she should again submit to be examined. I pacified her as well as I could, assuring her there was no help for it, but this was the last exposure her modesty would suffer. A pearly tear or two dropped from her lovely eyes, but she submitted. I withdrew the clothes whilst Hassan laid hold of her legs by the ankles, gently dividing them; the bottom of her lily thighs and the sheet were covered with crimson drops; the delicious entrance in the grove of Venus, which before she had received my luxurious stretches had so much the appearance of the bud of the rose, now hung flabby, loose and inflamed by the tremendous friction it had suffered, satisfying the beholder in a moment that the hymen had been broken and the deflowering completed. Hassan immediately bowed his head as satisfied and I conducted him out of the boudoir. On my return to her she was still in tears, but I soon dried them. Having ordered dinner, I told her a slave would attend to help her dress, and by the time her toilet was finished the meal would be ready. I sent by the slave a beautiful white satin dress, with diamond eardrops and pearl necklace and with a letter stating it was my wish she would wear these ornaments as a marriage gift.

'I waited her approach in the outer room. She came leaning on a slave. Her appearing to be scarcely able to walk caused me to fly to her support and her head sank on my shoulder unresistingly. I carried her to a couch, where throwing my arms around her, I drew her to my bosom and placing numerous soft kisses on her lips and neck, bestowed on her every endearing tide I could give utterance to. But although she trembled, blushed and sighed, and could hardly keep her eyes open, still, to my great gratification, her lips returned my soft pressures, and altogether there was something in her behaviour that satisfied me I had created an interest in her feelings that was tantamount to reciprocation; indeed every moment had the effect of removing the natural coyness which every girl must feel in the company of the happy possessor of her virginity so shortly after the loss. Dinner was served, of which she partook with apparent satisfaction. During our repast I caught her examining me when she thought I was engaged or did not observe her; her cheeks, neck and shoulders were instantly suffused with blushes on her discovering I had remarked what she was about. I tenderly drew her to my bosom, assuring her there was no reason for her blushes. In short the repast was enjoyed with double zest by me from the numerous nameless delicate pleasures I received from the maidenly confusion caused by the novelty of the situation in the lovely girl. After the banquet was removed it was past sunset. As she lay in my arms her eyes seemed heavy, which induced me to ask if she would retire and snatch an hour or two of repose before I came to pass the night with her, at the same time telling her she must not expect to get much sleep that night. She agreed to avail herself of my offer, on which, summoning the slave to assist her to undress, I supported her to the entrance of the boudoir, there resigning her into the slave's hands and giving instructions to leave all the lamps burning and properly supplied with oil.

'After reposing on a couch for about two hours I undressed myself. On entering the boudoir, I saw that Theodora slept naked from the heat of the weather; in her sleep she had removed nearly all the bedclothes. Her head lay on one of her arms on the pillow, her other arm lying carelessly by her side, whilst the treasures of her lovely breasts and shoulders were unprotected by the slightest covering. Without disturbing her, I laid myself by her side, bringing my mouth as nearly as possibly to hers. Our lips at last touched for a moment. I sucked her balmy breath. Lying thus examining the beauties of her delicate limbs, suddenly I perceived a strange confusion seem to seize upon her. She appeared as if struggling with someone; then she sighed. I caught the flying dream and gave her another soft kiss; still she slept. Her sweet disorder and struggles seemed to increase; she uttered some words, broken and inarticulate. A blush spread itself on her face and bosom; she turned upon her back as if impelled by the agency of someone, her lovely thighs spread of themselves, her breasts heaved rapidly, her whole body was agitated, her arms spread then of a sudden fell, and then she became motionless as death. Certainly she had tasted in a dream all those joys which the waking sense can know. A soft emotion succeed the calm in which she had been absorbed. "Yes, thou lovest me," she sighed, in the most tender accents; then sighed, breathed short, and again said, "Oh, I cannot doubt it."

'More lost in transport even than she, I had not power to move. A moment afterwards she became no less confounded than myself; her soul seemed to give itself up to an ecstasy; again she trembled and seemed convulsed with pleasure. Mahomet, how beautiful she appeared! How infinitely did this confusion become her! I could bear it no longer, but seized her in my arms and thus broke in upon her joys by awakening her—thereafter there remained no more of the illusion that had engrossed her faculties than that tender languishment to which she had abandoned herself with a warmth that rendered her worthy of the pleasures she had possessed. When she opened her eyes, where love itself reigned, the glances she darted appeared still full of the fire that was diffused through her veins; she had not yet lost the impression that had been made in her sleeping fancy. Oh, how touching was her very look. "Theodora," I cried, with rapture, pressing her to my bosom, "lovely, amiable Theodora, how beautiful you appeared just now," kissing her with all the ardour I was capable of expressing. The dream still retained some influence over her waking mind, the memory of her late impulse insensibly increased upon her, and desires to which she had hitherto been a stranger thrilled in her veins.

'Experienced as I am in womankind, my passion for Theodora now not only made me attentive to all her motions but also enabled me to make true conjectures as to their meaning. I saw quite enough to convince me I was not an object of indifference to her, and that now more than ever she regarded me with pleasure. The charming girl, altogether artless and sincere by nature, knew not how to disguise her thoughts; so if she did not tell me all she felt in my favour, it was only because of a shamefacedness. However, I discovered everything I wished to know, since I was alive to a consciousness of something more than her modesty would let her speak. But my kisses and touches, combined with her dream, now began to warm her. She now blushed less at every liberty I took than she had done before at those she apprehended I should take. In fact, in spite of herself she was beginning to partake of my transport. Whilst I was sucking her soft lips my hand slipped between her thighs but although it was between them still she kept them closed. "How is this," I cried, "lovely Theodora; do you refuse to make me happy again?" "Ah," she replied, unthinkingly, "you were but too much so just now, and before you awoke me had all the advantage you could wish." On pressure to explain the seeming mystery her words contained, she held out against my entreaties longer than I expected she would. Kisses and caresses, however, got the better of her in the end, and her reluctance to speak of the subject vanished by degrees. "If I should tell you," she said in a trembling voice, "do not abuse me." I swore I would not, but with transports which instead of removing her apprehension might have assured her it would be impossible for me to keep my promise. Too little skilled in mankind to be sensible of the effect of what she was about to reveal, she at least confessed to me that being in a slumber the moment before I spoke to her, she had seen me in a dream, and through my agency she felt a rapture which before she had notice of. 'Was I between your thighs?' cried I, pressing her strenuously in my arms. Covered with blushes but looking on me with eyes swimming with languor, she tremblingly replied, "Yes." "Ah, then," rejoined I, more inflamed, "You love me more in the idea than you do in my real person?" "That," she said, "would be impossible—I could not love you more; but it is certain I was less ashamed to tell you so." "But what more?" impatiently demanded I. "Oh, ask me not," replied she, hiding her blushes on my bosom; "I cannot enter in particulars; but I was indeed happy without regret." Here she paused for a moment, and then added, "or pain."


'Whilst she was thus explaining the effect of her dream I had extended her thighs, and with my forefinger for a few moments had been tickling the inside of her delicious love-sheath. Her eyes were turned full on me, charged with all the fires of love and soft desire, plainly intimating what her thoughts were. It was impossible longer to restrain my burning impatience, so turning her on her back, I got between her thighs, and laying myself on her, entreated her to say she loved me. She only answered with sighs, more impressive than words. I read in every look and motion what she would have said if not restrained by shame. One arm held her lips to mine, the other hand directed the instrument which in her dream had made her so happy. Faint murmurings and half-stifled sighs combating with the remains of modesty rendered her if possible more beautiful than ever, whilst with energy my vigorous instrument was driven up till it was at the end of its penetration, its progress sending up through her eyes the sparks of the love fire that now blazed in every vein—aye, in every pore in her. She had now taken in love's arrow (from the point to the feather) in that part where, now causing no pain, the lips, which owed their first breathing to my potent instrument, clung as if sensible of gratitude in eager suction around it with a warmth of zest, a compressive energy that gave it in its way the most delicious welcome in nature, every part of her sheath gathering tight around me, and straining as it were to come in for its blissful touch. Buried in her this way, we were both lost in an ecstasy and forgetfulness of ourselves or of what further was requisite to satisfy the demands of nature. We seemed to breathe out our whole souls upon each other's lips.

'We lay motionless through excess of bliss. After languishing for some moments on her bosom, I at length recovered, but the lovely girl could not bear the fierceness of my glances, and moved her head a little on one side, with a sigh breathing nothing but love. "Ah, Theodora," I softly exclaimed, "surely you did not in your dream turn away those swimming eyes, those soft lips?" at the same time trying if it were possible to strain myself further into her. Suddenly her arms encircled my neck, her lips joined mine with soft thrilling pressures, whilst with voluptuous activity she moved her young body to receive my thrusts, murmuring with tenderness, "Does that content you, dear sir?—is it thus?—how else can I act to satisfy you?' I had now no command of myself. Holy Mahomet, how wild was ecstasy. The soft joy had seized upon her senses, her tremblings, heaving, soft shudders, the active movements of her arms and legs, quick breathings, graspings, return of my kisses, all bespoke her dream realised. But nature, unable to support the torrent of pleasure, deserted us both: we sank insensible in each other's arms.

'I need not trouble you or excite your jealousy with any further account of the amorous scenes which took place between us. Long before morn she became (if anything) more submissive to my wishes than you were on your education. In the morning as she lay on my bosom, half asleep, moaning from the lassitude which a fierce enjoyment had just thrown her into, she suddenly sighed out, "Poor Emily!" I instantly comprehended the subject her thoughts were wandering on, particularly as a tear escaped from beneath her beautiful eyelid, rolled over her cheek and fell on my bosom. Pretending great alarm, I anxiously enquired the cause of her sorrow, when in the fullness of her grief she related the whole circumstances of the letter she had received from you, nor did she conceal (as she did in her first relation) the unkind reply she had written, which she now much regretted. "How could I," said she fondly, hiding her face in my bosom, "a poor silly maid as I was then, have any imagination of the transports I have tasted in your arms tonight? But it was very cruel to write to her as I did. Are you sure that the Dey ordered her to be strangled?" "Why," I replied, "there was a report that an English slave had been strangled; but there is no relying on anything we hear as to what takes place in the seraglio, even if it comes from the eunuchs themselves; there is so much deception carried on in respect of the Dey's women." "Indeed?" she sighed. "Yes," I continued, "if by any chance the letter you mention should have fallen into the Dey's hands, there is no danger, trouble or expense that would have deterred him from getting possession of your lovely person, and every artifice would have been used until he had enjoyed your virginity; and if he could not have enjoyed you by your own consent or deceit, he would not scruple in using force for the satisfying of his desires." "How can he expect anyone to love him?" she tenderly enquired. "It is reported," said I, "that very few women can resist him long, so well does he know how to please them. Besides, you do not form a true estimate of the power of man over the passions of women. Yesterday you were an ignorant maid who scarcely knew me! Now how many times during the night have your lips with the sweetest caresses called on your God as a witness to your love of me, whom a few short hours ago you had never seen before? Is it not true,?" said I fondly kissing her. "It is," she replied, throwing her arms around my neck "But though at our marriage there was no reason for love on my side, either my gratitude or what you have taught me since yesterday have engendered it, and certainly the Dey would not have made me feel as I do towards you now." This tender avowal again forced my almost unbounded passions; I clasped her with transport to my bosom, our lips joined, our breaths mingled; when gently I turned her on her back, her swelling thighs, now obedient to the intimations of love and nature, willingly extended, resigning up the gateway to the entrance of pleasure. Dividing the pouting lips and entering its velvet tip, the member was quickly wedged into her to its extremity—she had it now to her heart's content—ravished to its utmost capacity by being so. Stretched as she was almost to suffocation on a rack of pleasure, its point stung her so much that catching at length the rage from my furious driving, she went wholly out of her mind, her sense concentrating in that favourite part of her body, the whole of which was so luxuriously filled and employed. There alone she existed, all lost in those delicious transports, those ecstasies of the senses, which her winking eyes, the brightened vermilion of her lips and sighs of pleasure deeply fetched so pathetically expressed. In short she was a machine (like any other piece of machinery) obeying the impulses of the key that so potently set her in motion, till the sense of pleasure foaming to a height triggered the shower that was to allay this hurricane. She kept me faithful company, going off with the old symptoms-a delicious delirium, a tremulous shudder, an "Ah, me, where am I?" and two or three long sighs, followed by the critical, dying, "Oh, oh!" When I got off her, she lay motionless, pleasure-filled—stretched and drenched—quite spent and gasping for breath, without any other sensations of life than in those exquisite vibrations that trembled yet on the strings of delight which had been so ravishingly touched and which nature had too intensely striven with for the senses to be quickly at peace from. 'In this manner did I gratify my senses and take my revenge on the lovely Theodora for the insult paid to me. Thus she became the slave of my pleasures. She little knew the effect of the storm she was raising and how potently she would feel it when it exploded. Having deposited in her womb my burning revenge, I was satisfied, and all that now remained was to undeceive her and to introduce you. It did not require much ingenuity to bring this about. Foreseeing clearly there would be a few pearly tears shed between you, also that I should have to listen to a few tender reproaches from Theodora, this also was no great matter. Having devoted nearly three weeks to the enjoyment of Theodora, yesterday I intended to withdraw the curtain which hung before her eyes. I desired Hassan at a particular hour to bring you to the apartments of Theodora, and when he heard me use a particular expression to let you enter the boudoir. It is scarcely necessary to explain that Theodora was now brought to submit to every, indeed any, wish I could form. On this occasion I had stripped her entirely naked, having nothing but a loose robe on myself. In this state I directed her to lean on the couch with her face downwards, raising her a little by placing a footstool for each foot to stand on at some distance from each other, so that her thighs were properly extended, and the entrance perfectly exposed. The head of my instrument was then fixed in her. At this moment you entered according to my directions, but dress disguised you so much that she did not know you, and Hassan caught you as you fainted. I motioned for him to take you away, then immediately resheathed the weapon in her hungry gap, as I well knew that would suppress all enquiry regarding you for the present. I seized her round the loins and demanded of her if she should like to be placed in that situation with the Dey. She turned round her head, with evident fear of some unknown danger marked in her lovely face, and replied, "Ah, sir, you make me tremble." "Why should you tremble, sweet one? He has been often near you during the last weeks and is at this moment nearer than you suppose." "Oh, where," cried the visibly alarmed girl, "where is he?" "Why up to your very quick," was my reply, and I forced myself into her as far as I could go. "It is the Dey who has enjoyed your virginity, whose wife you suppose yourself to be, and whom you now feel up to the hilt in your vitals." She fainted, but my violent thrusts soon brought her to life. The ecstasy seized me, I discharged myself into her, and withdrawing from her exclaimed, "There, my child, the deception is finished, you now know the beast in all his beastliness. Know, sweet charmer," I exclaimed, "it was that letter of yours that has procured the pleasure you have received in my embraces; the female that just now interrupted us is your friend Emily." To this she uttered a faint scream and fainted again. As I was ready for action I was soon in her again, and a few fierce thrusts quickly brought her to. To be brief, while my instrument was in her I had no difficulty in obtaining her pardon. She entreated permission to fly to you, and I granted her request. The rest you know.'

As the Dey ceased speaking his rampant tool (which I must confess I was handling during his confession) gave tokens of preparation and soon I had the delicious morsel where I fain would have kept it forever. After this the Dey would often amuse himself with us alternately, compelling one of us to guide into the other his instrument and handle his pendant jewels; then he would throw his hand back and insert his finger into the gaping place that awaited its turn. In this way we were frequently (all three) dissolved at the same time in a flood of bliss. This had continued for several weeks, when an awful catastrophe put an end to our enjoyments. The Dey had received a Greek girl from one of his captains. She passively submitted to his embraces, and uttered no complaint until he commenced the attack upon her second maidenhead; then did she seem inspired with the strength of a Hercules. She suddenly seized a knife, which she had concealed under a cushion, grasped his pinnacle of strength, and in less than a thought drew the knife across it and severed it from his body, she then plunged it into her own heart and expired immediately.

Aid was immediately summoned to stop the Dey's bleeding to death, and with the fortitude that ever characterises greatness, he ordered his physician to relieve him of his now useless remaining appendages, his receptacles of the soul-stirring juice, remarking at the same time that life would be hell if he retained the desire after the power was dead. When the Dey had nearly recovered he sent for us, and disclosed to our view the lost members preserved in spirits of wine in glass vases. He affectionately bade us farewell, telling us that a ship would sail for England in a few days, and as he had no further use for us, he would send us back to our native land. His kindness had such an effect on my feelings as to cause a miscarriage. I lay dangerously ill for two weeks, during which time Sylvia attended me with the care of a mother. At length the time of departure arrived. The Dey sent for us, and presented one of his valuable vases to Sylvia and the other to me. It fell to my lot to have the shaft. He also made us several other valuable presents, and bade us farewell, hoping that in our own country we should find partners to supply him. We left him with a heavy heart. We embarked on board the ship and arrived here without accident. Our friends here hushed up matters and reported that we had been at a boarding school in France, instead of the boarding school of the Dey of Algiers. Sylvia afterwards married a baronet, who lost his charge before he effected his entrance, so well did she play the prude. As for myself, you well know what my sentiments are. I will never marry until I am assured that the chosen one possesses sufficient charm and weight not only to erase the Dey's impression from my heart, but also from a more sensitive part. I have a young willing maid who possesses wiles enough to catch any man, and sufficient experience to answer my purpose; out of ten suitors, seven have passed through her ordeal and been found wanting. My hopes at present are centred on an Irish earl, who I have a presentiment will be found worthy of acceptance. When I have changed my name, rest assured you shall know the particulars.

You no doubt wish to know what became of the vases, therefore I must ease your mind on that score. Sylvia has a female friend who keeps a fashionable boarding school in London, and she persuaded me to leave mine with hers in the keeping of this lady, who shows them as a reward for good behaviour to the little lady scholars. Poor girls, how their little mousetraps must gape at the sight!

EMILY BARLOW

THE END